Stone of Hope

by

Margaret Izard

Stones of Iona, Book Four

Contact Information: info@thewildrosepress.com

Cover Art by *Lisa Dawn MacDonald*

The Wild Rose Press, Inc.
PO Box 708
Adams Basin, NY 14410-0708
Visit us at www.thewildrosepress.com

Publishing History
First Edition, 2025
Trade Paperback ISBN 978-1-5092-5959-5
Digital ISBN 978-1-5092-5960-1

Stones of Iona, Book Four
Published in the United States of America

Dedication

To my kids, the "triple latte's" who aren't "hell on earth" but damned fun. What a ride! To my husband for all his love and support. Thank you for our adventure of raising our "little hellions" and all the fun along the way.

Chapter 1

Never forget, words are not the reality. Only reality is reality. Picture symbols are the idea. Words are confusion.

Evie MacDougall tiptoed past the familiar entry to the Egyptian display in the National Museum of Science in Miami, Florida, as her brother Ewan bumped into her. "Shhh, Ma will find us." Douglas and his younger sister, Katherine, better known as Kat, brought up the rear of the entourage. Doug, Ewan's ever-present shadow and all-time co-conspirator, kept a lookout in case either mother found them in the newer section of the museum—forbidden for them to enter and *oh so tempting* for the teens.

Evie moved along as she whispered to her brother, "Don't want Ma to catch us. She's busy setting up her display."

Doug followed, holding his younger sister Kat's hand. "Yeah, my ma would tan my hide if she found us in here."

Ewan turned and hissed, "Tanned hides. Ha! My da's wallop is harder than yers."

Colin MacDougall, their da and laird, were along for this trip with Evie's ma, Brielle, plus Doug and Kat's ma, Marie. The three adults weare next door setting up Evie's ma's newest display on Scottish history and lore from their home, Dunstaffnage Castle,

Scotland.

It was not only a setup of one stop on the museum tour but also a chance for the entire family to visit Uncle Dom, Dominic DeVolt, her mother's brother, who was Air Force Special Ops, and the most adventurous uncle Evie could ever hope for.

As Evie peered into the display, her twin brother Ewan stepped behind her. "I don't get what ye see in this part of the museum. Egypt is less fun than Scotland, and everything is even older."

Kat moved closer to Ewan.

As he kept a look out, Doug bumped into her.

Keeping her eyes on the Egyptian display, Evie replied to her brother. "It is because it's older that makes it that much more interesting, brother."

Ewan rolled his eyes but peered into the display as his sister crept from around the statue of Horus and approached the large, major attraction—the Eye of Ra.

Evie loved this part of the museum; the artifacts traveled with them from Houston to Florida for another tour stop, and she would have the chance to spend more time with them.

Her eyes traveled over to the storyboard display of Moira White. Her story amazed Evie. The youthful thirteen-year-old admired the young woman from the past who, in her early twenties, single-handedly led her hired crew, excavating one of the largest tombs in Egypt—the tomb of Sheshonq II, a previously unknown northern king. The wealth found rivaled Tutankhamun's find.

Ewan came and stood beside her. "Ye are always staring at her. Why?"

"She's inspiring. Her uncle raised her after she lost

her family, yet she still became successful even when that French archeologist, Pierre Lenoir, stole her digs after her uncle died. Pierre even accused her of stealing his notes, which led to her notable discovery. Then she mysteriously disappeared." She sighed. "I feel it in my bones. Pierre was a liar and a cheat regardless of how history wrote the story."

Evie glanced at the picture of Moira White, who stood on a flat surface that appeared to be part of the top of a pyramid in Egypt. The woman had her back half to the camera, so the side of her face showed over her shoulder. She stood overlooking the valley in Cairo with the Nile River flowing through. She was so high up from the river that it looked like a small ribbon. She wore black peep-toe pumps with a white cotton 1930s day dress. She'd pulled her hair back in the flapperesque style with set curls on her forehead. The shot seemed to catch her just as she turned to the camera to say something witty.

Evie's gaze traveled back to the Eye of Ra. The artifact drew her since she'd first spied it months ago. Like a moth to the flame, she had to see it again.

Her comrades, now more confident on their concealed adventure, crept closer as Evie stood staring at the large golden eye with black details painted to depict the infamous Eye of Ra.

Kat, Evie's best friend forever, stood beside her, staring into the eye. "I don't understand why ye want to stare at an eye constantly. It creeps me out." She shivered. "It's like it's looking at me."

Ewan groaned. "That's because it *is*."

He pinched Kat. She squealed loudly.

As it echoed throughout the museum, Evie and

Doug loudly sputtered, "Shhh."

Evie turned back to the Eye of Ra and felt something pull in her. She couldn't define it, but this feeling drew her in as if it tried to tell her something.

Evie closed her eyes and opened her mind to the sensation. Blessed with Fae's powers, Evie secretly worked with Brigid, the family Fae assigned to the MacDougall family, to help protect the Stones of Iona, to hone and control her powers—something the Fae gave to few humans. And her activities her parents didn't know she did in secret. Brigid always told her to focus on the strongest feeling, the one trying to reach her, which spoke the loudest.

Hope echoed, so she focused on hope. Warmth spread through her. Her arms rose of their own accord, reaching for the Eye of Ra. As she opened her eyes, all in the room gasped. In the center of the eye was a picture. She tilted her head to the side, and it wasn't just a picture; it was a movie.

A woman bent over the sarcophagus, brushing sand with a large brush while humming. The wall behind her resembled the picture in the Egyptian display, filled with shapes and figures lined up in rows. Light cast her room on a soft yellow glow, and light's shadows danced across the wall behind her as if a slight breeze had shifted candlelight. The woman turned to speak to someone, and the kids got their first glimpse of whom they spied on.

Ewan spoke from beside her. "I'll be damned. That's the lady. The one in the display, the White lady."

Doug froze, staring, but it was Kat who spoke. "Isn't she from the 1930s? Why are we seeing her movie in the eyeball?"

Evie shook her head. "It's not a movie, Kat. It's her in real life." Evie gasped as reality hit her. "Guys, I found a portal, a Fae time portal to Egypt. But Egypt of the 1930s."

Ewan grabbed her arms. "Close it, Evie. Ye have to close it." He pulled and turned her to him.

When her brother turned her, she lost contact with the eye. The movie disappeared. The portal closed. Dazed, Evie frowned at her brother, her lifelong friend and confidant.

A tear escaped and trailed down her cheek. "God, Ewan, ye can't tell. I didn't mean to open it. It just happened."

Ewan hugged her. "It's okay, Evie." He glared at Doug and Kat. "We tell no one. It's our secret."

Doug and Kat nodded, speaking together. "Aye."

****

Colin stood back as his wife placed the last artifact, completing the display for Dunstaffnage's Chapel in the Woods. It was Brielle's first major historical project and her proudest work. Not that it had anything to do with how she met her true love and made their perfect family.

She stood in the life-sized partial replica of the decorative historical chapel when he approached, wrapped his muscular arms around his wife's tiny waist, and whispered in her ear, "Every time ye build this, I get goose bumps standing in it no matter where we are." He kissed her ear and trailed kisses down her neck, enticing a shiver. "Makes me want ye all over again as if we had just met and fallen in love for the first time."

She turned in his arms and kissed him. "Husband, I

5

feel the same way."

Marie strode into the display and stood next to them. "If ye two keep that up, we'll never finish setting up the display. Then we'll miss dinner with Dominic."

Bree glanced around, moving out of the chapel replica. "Speaking of dinner, where are the kids?"

Colin followed not far behind and spotted the group of teens entering the Scottish display from the side. A side they should not be coming from. Not saying anything, he caught his son Ewan's eye and nodded to the side. Telling him to move along before their mother found out they were in the forbidden area.

Colin loudly spoke as he traveled opposite from the group of wayward teens. "I'm sure they are here, just behind something. Ye have added so many more artifacts over the years. I wonder if ye left anything at Dunstaffnage or if the grounds will be the same."

Bree turned to him. "We returned all the soil and landscaping, Colin. You know this."

He smiled and caressed her face, then deeply kissed her. Something he enjoyed more over time.

A long groan interrupted the kiss. "Eww, do they ever stop?" Doug leaned against the display of the Viking longboat found close to Dunstaffnage Castle. Marie and Bree found it a couple of years ago and suspected it might be the burial spot of Ainslie's husband, Rannick, who lived in the Viking times. Ainslie was Colin's sister, who had traveled back in time to the Vikings on the trip to save Brielle from the evil Fae, where they recovered the Stone of Lust for safekeeping. Colin didn't favor thinking of the Viking time trip, a hard one for Bree. And one where he'd left his sister in the past with her true love. The boat was a reminder that his sister wasn't alive. He preferred to think of her as living in Viking time—but now.

Marie barked, scolding her son. "No, and don't lean on the exhibit. That boat is old."

Doug shrugged. "Yeah, Ma, I get it. Everything here is old."

Marie hugged her son. "Ye should consider yerself so lucky, friends and parents who are in love."

Kat walked by her ma and brother. "I think it's romantic how everyone found their true loves. I hope to do that someday."

Doug huffed a laugh. "Ye'll be lucky to find yer sock for yer shoe in the morning before ye find true love."

Kat hit her brother, and short fisticuffs ensued. Marie stepped between the two, wrangling them to a stop.

Noting she stood off to the side, Colin approached his daughter during the chaos. "Ye're quiet today, Evie. Anything wrong?" He kept a closer eye on his daughter since the last time the Fae were active when they recovered a Stone of Iona. The family recovered the stones of Love, Fear, and Lust for the good Fae. Still not recovered were Hope, Faith, Doubt, and Destiny. It'd been years since anything last occurred. After the previous encounter with the Fae, he and Bree closely watched their twins, Evie and Ewan. Brigid, the family Fae, blessed the twins with Fae powers. Something Colin wasn't happy with but learned to live with over time. While Evie's powers had surfaced instantly, Ewan's hadn't, and Colin hoped to keep it that way.

Evie shocked him and Bree the first time she displayed Fae powers when she separated Bree's Iona

Stone in half and magically merged it again, whole. Brigid told her it was a power she would need in the future, a future yet to occur.

Evie peeked at her da and blushed. "Nothing, Da. Just tired, I guess."

Colin gathered his teen daughter in his arms and squeezed her once. Something he often did to convey his love for her without using embarrassing words the teen found awkward but craved all the same. "Ahh, I suspect there may be more to it than ye're just tired, but I'll allow it to slide. We have to get going to meet Uncle Dom."

Evie peeked at her father and grinned.

He placed his finger on her nose and bent close. "Ye'd be less tired if ye stayed away from the Egyptian display, Evie."

She gasped.

Colin covered it up by announcing, "Time to go. Our visit with Dom has been long coming. Let's head out to dinner; I'm famished."

Everyone filed out of the museum, the evening early, and a promise of a fun time with the favored Uncle Dom.

Chapter 2

Dominic stood at the back of the room, done out of pure habit. Survey all the activity and assess any threat. He smirked. There would likely be no threat at a museum tour opening reception, but one never knew.

He stood leaning against the wall in his button-down white shirt open at the collar with his legs crossed in his pressed black pants. He hated dress shoes and had black boots, which looked like dress shoes but were combat boots favored by his special ops team. He flipped his tousled medium brown hair and shifted his shoulders, relaxing into the night. He had opted for street clothes, as the Air Force uniform drew attention. He wanted his sis to be the star tonight.

The last time he stood in a museum reception, his sister's ex-boyfriend attacked and abducted her. His gaze sought her out and found her on the arm of her hulky, protective Scottish husband, Colin. Nothing would happen to Brielle. Her husband would see to it. Dominic smiled. He liked the overbearing Scot, who was totally in love with his sister. And she with him.

Dom and his sister had grown apart, but after she moved to Scotland, he traveled off and on to get to know her better. Things went much better after her abduction at the hands of her ex, possessed by the head of the Evil Fae. He exhaled. The ex was dead at the hands of Colin.

He caught her beam up at her husband. His big sis had grown into quite a woman, charming and outspoken. Plus, she was very successful at her passion, Scottish history. He stood in an entire wing of Florida's Science Museum filled with her finds, some of Scotland's greatest historical treasures. Today was her day.

He eyed the couple again as they kissed. True love—the two claimed they were fated mates. He chuckled at the thought; fated love. Dominic had dated a few women. For the most part, they were nice, but nothing as earth-shattering as what Bree and Colin had. He sighed as he recalled a conversation with Bree about fated love.

Bree smirked at him. "Dom, don't you believe in true love?"

He sneered at his big sis. "No, not really. Love is something found in the clouds. Relationships are work." He tapped his finger on her chin and peered down at his shorter big sis. "The type of work and complications someone like me has little time for."

Bree batted his finger away. "Trust me, brother. I thought something similar." She glanced away. "I thought love was lost to me, thanks to my ex." She looked back at him. "But it hit me unexpectedly from the most unlikely of places." She pushed her finger into his chest. "It will hit you too, trust me. And it will be when you least expect it."

For true love to find him, it'd have to be something pretty extraordinary.

A tall, attractive blonde woman walked by and eyed him from head to toe.

She stopped, raising an eyebrow. "Do these things

bore you as much as they bore me?"

Dominic grunted. "No." Nothing his sister did bored him. She was an amazing woman.

He spotted a movement behind the partial life-sized Chapel in the Woods model from Dunstaffnage Castle, one of Bree and Colin's homes.

He stepped past the woman. "Excuse me."

He slipped alongside the faux wall and peered around the corner. The figure disappeared down a corridor close to their private event. Dominic casually eased his way toward the hallway marked Hall of Ancient Egypt.

Dominic spotted four familiar teens from around the corner in the Egyptian exhibit.

Ewan pulled his twin sister's arm. "Evie, we are going to get into trouble. Come on. Let's go back."

Evie shook his arm off and approached the Eye of Ra.

Doug wrestled with his younger sister, Kat, trying to keep her from climbing on the chariot with the life-sized plastic horses.

Ewan stood next to Evie and kept looking back to the hall from which they had just come.

"I can't help myself, Ewan. The eye. It calls me."

Ewan snorted. "Well, don't answer. We need to get back before Ma and Da find us missing."

Kat fell into the chariot, and Doug climbed in as Ewan called, "Doug, ye guys need to get off the displays. Both our mas will have our necks if we break anything."

Dominic slid behind the display of a mummy in a sarcophagus. The kids knew better than to play on the presentations. Dominic grabbed the fake corpse's arm, not missing an opportunity to have a little fun, preparing to play another prank.

Ewan turned back to Evie when Dominic made the carcass raise a hand as he moaned loudly.

"Mmmmmmmm." Between the legs of the coffin's stand, he spotted the kids. This was priceless.

Ewan grabbed Evie's hand, and she grabbed his shoulders. Inside the chariot, Doug stood frozen, and Kat disappeared as she likely huddled down. Dominic had difficulty not laughing and spoiling the surprise.

He shook the mummy's hand toward Evie and Ewan as he spoke deeply. "You naughty children should not play with my display."

Evie and Ewan screamed as they hugged each other.

The hand dropped, and he popped up from behind the sarcophagus, smiling widely.

Evie spoke as she sagged against her brother, "Oh God, Uncle Dom!"

Ewan dropped his hands from Evie's shoulders and stood with them fisted at his sides, looking much like his father, Colin.

Dominic laughed as he came from around the casket. Bree's kids were a handful, that was for sure. As toddlers, they'd called the twins "little hellions." As teenagers, they were hell on earth. God, they were fun.

Ewan spoke as Doug and Kat scrambled out of the chariot. "That's not funny, Uncle Dom."

Still laughing, Dominic came closer to the twins. "Maybe not, but your expressions were priceless." He scanned the room out of habit. "What are you kids doing here, anyway? Aren't you supposed to be back with the Scottish display?" He breathed. All clear.

When his eyes returned, Doug and Kat stood by the chariot, eyeing the ground and holding each other's hand.

Ewan stood by Evie. "Evie wanted to come to see the eye. It's an obsession of hers."

Dominic stood watching Evie, who gazed at the Eye of Ra. He turned and studied the eye, noting how large the golden artifact was. The pupil alone had to be four feet in diameter, and the whole eye was around ten feet wide. The value of the gold alone staggered his mind. He noted there was little to no extra security around the object, which was strange.

His eye caught on the large display beside it, and a life-sized black-and-white picture of a woman stared back at him. His breath caught as the woman was of startling beauty. Her expression was one of mocking challenge.

He took a step toward her. "Who is she?" In the black-and-white photo, she was beautiful. In color, he wondered what color her hair would be—dark for sure based upon the shading, but those highlights. Red maybe?

Ewan came up beside him. "She's cool, isn't she? She found all this stuff."

Dominic read the display out loud. "In 1939, Moira Joanna White literally struck gold. On February twenty-seventh, she found a king's tomb, identified by inscriptions as Osorkon II. There were several rooms, but thieves plundered everything. Remaining in a sealed room, however, was a fabulous quartzite sarcophagus for Osorkon's son, Takelot II; hundreds of *ushabtis*, figurines of servants that would magically come to life and serve the pharaoh in the next world; alabaster jars;

and other objects."

Ewan cleared his throat. "Let me save ye some time. She found another sealed tomb in addition to that one, but they'd marked it wrong. It was a king, Psusennes I, and this is some of his stuff, too. Everything here was from the ancient city of Tanis, in the Nile Delta northeast of Cairo."

Ewan walked to the presentation with a great silver head next to the coffin.

Dominic followed, unable to help his curiosity as Ewan picked up his commentary. "She found that the northern king's tomb, Osorkon II, was in the same area. The King of Egypt came when she opened it. They found this silver head and more jewelry. The archeological society claimed the find rivaled King Tutankhamun's tomb with its valuable riches and historical significance."

Dominic raised his eyebrows at Ewan. "You seem educated on this Moira lady."

Ewan sighed. "Well, Evie has spent a lot of time here. I don't want to leave her alone. Nothing to do but sit here and read."

Dominic gazed back at the picture of Moira. "So, what happened to her?" He peered over the display and read the last paragraph aloud.

"Pierre Lenoir accused Moira of stealing his notes and discovering the tombs using his research, which put her discovery in a long legal battle. He demanded the Egyptian courts turn over the discovery to his team, saying that a lone woman with a meager team of village riffraff could not have discovered such riches." He took a deep breath. "Tossing the situation into further turmoil, Miss White mysteriously disappeared shortly after the filing. The case remains unsolved, but they credited this finding to her alone."

"Moira Joanna White. She sure is pretty. Too bad she's dead."

Dominic turned toward the exit as Evie spoke. "Wanna see her in real life?"

He stopped and turned to Evie. "What?"

Evie looked at Dominic, then at the Eye of Ra.

Ewan stepped toward his sister as Dominic shot his hand out to stop him.

Ewan grabbed her shoulder. "Evie, don't."

Evie raised her hands. His ears buzzed, and the room filled with an electrified energy. He'd felt something like this on another assignment where he flew a unique craft. The "out of this world" one he couldn't tell anyone about. The overcharged sensation overwhelmed Dominic in the same way.

Evie shifted her hands, and the pupil of the Eye of Ra turned a little, then rotated. It spun faster and faster, swirling into a gray mass. As the gray of the center faded, a picture appeared as he stared, and the image moved.

Dominic stood transfixed. Before him was a movie of Moira White bent over a sarcophagus, cleaning it with a large brush. Her thick auburn hair caught the torchlight as dust particles flickered around her head. So, it *was* red. She turned as if someone had called her, making Dominic's breath escape in a whoosh. Before him was a full-color live version of the photo. The stunning beauty from the past, alive before his eyes.

As she gave him a full smile, he moved forward, tilting his head. He returned the grin, completing the connection. The picture rotated off-center, and the air traveled around him. The ringing came back to his ears, louder.

A kid's gasp came from behind as Ewan screamed, "Evie, what's wrong? What's happening?"

Dominic turned. Ewan held Evie's shoulders as she gasped for air and held her hands out to the eye. The wind picked up and swirled around them as the picture inside the eye's pupil rotated faster.

Evie yelled over the wind, "I can't control it, Ewan! It's got a hold of me! I can't stop it!"

The churning wind dragged Evie toward the eye as Ewan grasped her shoulders, trying to push her away. A gust of wind pressed the twins, and they slid fast toward Dominic. When they slammed into him, his reflexes took over, and he grabbed them. He held both teenagers in his arms, trying to push them away from the eye.

Dominic searched for Doug and Kat and found they'd taken cover behind the chariot. Thank God he'd got only two to worry over.

He yelled over the wind, "Doug, keep Kat safe. Stay there."

Ewan cried out, "Evie, ye have to stop it! Close yer eyes! Shut it off!"

Tears streamed down Evie's face. "I can't. I'm frozen!" *This can't be!* The eye dragged them toward it. The energized force pulled as Dominic tried to push away. Whatever this was, Dominic feared it was not good.

Dominic yelled over the wind, "Hold on, kids. I've got you!" He gathered them both in his arms as he fought to keep them from the eye. The wind hit them with a forceful blow, and all three flew into the Eye of Ra.

****

After they disappeared, the eye's swirl disappeared. The wind stopped as fast as it began. The room sat in silence.

Doug and Kat came out from behind the chariot. Doug glanced around. Evie, Ewan, and Uncle Dom were gone. The Eye of Ra sucked them into Egypt. Egypt of the past.

Doug squinted at his sister. "Shit, we're in big trouble now."

****

The other side of the portal, Egypt, 1939

"Nubi, hand me the other brush. I think I found another set of hieroglyphics." Moira reached her hand out as dust fell from the sleeve of her shirt. It had once been white but now was covered in a brown dusting from the tomb's dirt. Multiple trips up and down the shaft had long ago stained her pants. As she brushed the sand away from the wall, colorful images appeared out of a timeless state of hidden wonder. Moira loved discovering untouched pieces of history. Nothing excited her more than the Egyptians.

A new chamber. Moira discovered a new section and suspected it was another son of Ramesses II in the Valley of the Kings. This would be it. The first registered find of her own, and it would solidify her place in archeological history—the first lone woman to discover a tomb. She couldn't turn her face away from the view before her, which was still intact even after rain damage to the tomb. Well, the bottom third was a loss, but this top part was exquisite.

Nubi handed her the smaller brush as a commotion broke out from the top of the shaft. "I'll check and see what the problem is. You keep working. Nubi take care of Miss."

Moira only nodded as she continued her examination of the paintings on the wall.

Nubi started up the narrow shaft. A yelp and a grunt sounded. Moira turned and faced a gun muzzle pointed at her nose.

"Bonjour, Moira. It seems we meet again." Pierre Lenoir's accent grated as he examined the small chamber. Moira followed his gaze. Nubi sat on the ground, also held at gunpoint by one of Pierre's thugs. Another peered down on the scene as it unfolded.

Moira's eyes went back, and she stared down the gun barrel and the man holding it as pure, heated hate flowed through her at the sight of her nemesis, Pierre Lenoir. He'd covered his black hair with the wax he liked, giving it a perfectly slicked-back look. His pale complexion was blotchy from the heat above, cooling now that they were underground. He still wore the perfectly pristine white suit with a small black tie. Not a smudge marred the fabric, and it never would. Pierre made others do his dirty work while he basked in the glory of success at the expense of slave labor. His eyes traveled over Moira like a starved Frenchman might look over a chocolate éclair. A chill spread down her spine as he spoke in his French accent, heavy and mocking.

"Why, look at what you have found, my dear. Another tomb in the Valley of Kings. Why, does this make it your *deuxième* or *troisième*?"

Moira huffed. She knew what Pierre's goal was, and she vowed not today. "Third. And the last one you will steal out from under me, from my family."

Pierre shook his head, tsking, but still held the gun pointed at her face. "Oh, my dear. So sorry to hear of your uncle's passing. Tragic circumstances lead to— accidents."

Moira raised her hand to wipe the dust from her face.

Pierre grabbed it. "Ah, ah, ah, dear. No sudden movements. Wouldn't want an *accident* happening again."

Pierre gripped her wrist and stepped closer as the gun went to her cheek. "Such a *jolie* thing. It would be such a waste." He wrestled her arm behind her back, twisting it, forcing Moira to arch her back.

Taking advantage of the position, Pierre rubbed his chest against hers. "A single young woman like yourself, alone in the world." He bent close as their breaths mingled. The onions he'd eaten soured her stomach.

Moira turned her head to the side, but Pierre used the gun barrel to force her to face him. "Join me, Moira. Let's be partners. I've always wanted you, even when your uncle was my partner. I always wanted the beautiful, young Moira." He kissed her lips and stayed connected, trying to insert his tongue into her mouth.

Moira kept her mouth shut. When he lifted his lips, she spat in his face.

Pierre's reaction came swiftly. He dropped her hand and slapped her hard. Moira kept her head turned from the force of the blow.

He flipped her around, shoving her into the wall, and pressed his body against her back. "Bitch, have it your way, then."

Pierre glanced to his thug in the shaft, speaking in

Margaret Izard

Arabic, "*Tamin al-haffar, wajma amalha. Lakchaf ho alaan ley.*" *Secure the dig and gather her workers. The find is now mine.*

Moira, understanding, struggled against his hold. "No, the find is mine. I registered it with the historical foundation. I have a permit and all. It's legal. I'm twenty-one. You can't take it from me."

Pierre ground his hips into her. His rock-hard erection dug into her rear, making Moira almost throw up.

Laughing, Pierre replied, "Silly girl, I've already taken it. Sadly, you didn't file the permit correctly. Tsk, tsk. I filed it when the authorities released it—for errors." Pierre leaned against her, whispering in her ear, "You should have taken my offer, girl. Now you lose it all, just like you lost your family."

****

Wind blew her face, and Moira shivered as the memory faded. Standing at a new dig in Tanis, Egypt, she took a fortifying breath. A day didn't go by she wasn't reminded of that dig, of what Pierre had done. If it weren't for Nubi and his village, New Gourna nearby, she'd never have made it out of the Valley of the Kings alive. They'd treated her like family, allowing her to stay until Pierre and his thugs left the valley. With *her find* packed and cataloged for filing *as his*.

It wasn't until that day that she learned of his true intent all those years ago when her uncle trusted him as his partner. All the times they'd lived in tent cities. The old man, Pierre, lusted after her. She shuddered as she shook off another chill.

That was five years ago, the last time Pierre stole a dig from her. Over time, she'd had many other projects,

20

minor compared to the Ramesses II son's tomb. Finds that were her own, under her name. She sighed and brushed her wayward hair away from her tanned face. The deep auburn curls were always unruly with a mind of their own.

She never returned to the United States after her parents' death. Uncle Ben had been a famous Egyptian archeologist and raised Moira on digs. Her uncle's death had rocked her world, tipping it upside down. She was always suspicious of the circumstances of his death. With Uncle Ben's death, she'd lost her last family and had to make her way at twenty-one.

Five years later and much wiser, she'd begun her next dig. One she hoped held the promise of a great find. Her eyes roamed the hills. Other archeologists who'd tried this area claimed it held no significance. But she felt differently. There were discrepancies in the tomb labeling. In her heart, she felt this would be the next significant archeological find.

She turned to Nubi and the men from his village she'd hired at trade rates, not slave rates like Pierre.

Taking a deep breath, she gave the order for her next dig. "Nubi, I feel it. We may discover something spectacular."

Nubi replied, "Aye, Miss Moira. Many treasures we already found. But today, we head to the newly opened chamber. The mismarked one." He waved her to the hole in the sand. "You'll be excited when you see."

Moira grinned, knowing he referred to the Divine Family Statue they'd found last week, which indicated the area was more significant than originally thought. She loved that statue—one of family.

She descended into the chamber, and Moira's anticipation built. Once inside, she found Ra's large golden eye. An indicator the tomb held someone of power. She moved quickly to the sarcophagus, sidestepping over the piles of offerings and belongings to the dead. Weapons and shields were in good condition, sitting beside long-rotted foodstuff, indicating that this was the pharaoh she had hoped it would be. Mismarked and untouched, she knew this was a great find. Hope welled within her as she whipped out her favorite brush and began the dirty work of clearing the sand.

As Moira brushed the dust off the coffin lid, a blast of wind blew through the chamber, followed by an enormous thump. She whipped around, fearful Nubi or a helper had fallen down the shaft.

The torches wavered, casting strange shadows on the hieroglyphic-covered walls.

Grunts and mumbling of more than one voice came from behind the casket. "Nubi, is that you?"

There was a distinctive sniffle of what sounded like a female who cried.

A strong masculine voice spoke. "Don't worry, kids. I've got you."

Moira went around the sarcophagus, and a man and two teenagers lay in a tangle of arms and legs. The man held the female cradled in his arms. The other teenager, a male, tried to stand while brushing sand off his clothing.

The male youth looked up. "Shit, it's her."

The man glanced up. "Language, Ewan. You are in the presence of a lady."

The male youth, Ewan, stepped back while the man

held a crying female teenager.

Moira moved forward. "Did you fall down the shaft? Are you hurt?" She bent down to help the man, and their eyes met. The most sparkling shade of light blue met hers, and she stopped as her breath caught. The female sniffled again, breaking the spell.

Moira helped the man as he scrambled to his knees to help the girl to her feet. "I'm sorry, Uncle Dom. I tried to hold it, but I couldn't."

She hiccupped a sniffle as Uncle Dom stood, rubbing her back. "It's okay, Evie. You did your best."

The man, Uncle Dom, examined the chamber as if seeing it for the first time. Moira figured she should be alarmed, but she wasn't. Hearing the youth call him uncle reminded her so much of her own that her heart went out to the female.

She peeked at the man again, Dom, and experienced an instant attraction to him. She had to step back in the closed quarters. Her desire to reach out and touch him was strong.

Dominic finally turned, gazing at her. He stood staring for a moment as if struck speechless.

Moira glimpsed down and cleared her throat before she spoke. "Dom, I think you fell down the shaft."

She eyed the three people in front of her. "Although I find it difficult to believe all three of you fell together. The shaft is barely big enough for one, let alone three."

Dominic kept his arm around the sniffling female. "I'm Dominic, and these are my niece and nephew, Evie and Ewan."

Ewan grinned. "We are twins. Ye are much prettier in person." Evie elbowed her brother as Dominic placed his hands on each of their shoulders, stilling them.

Moira gave a crooked smile. "Well, this is a strange way to meet, but I am Moira White." She nodded toward the shaft. "How about we all go topside where the air is better and see if we can sort this out?" She headed up the ladder and waved them to follow.

****

Dominic turned as he kept Evie in his arms. Behind them was the Eye of Ra—the same as the one in the future.

He bent, speaking softly to Evie, "Don't look at it. Keep your eyes closed." She squinted hard as Dominic steered her toward the ladder.

He leaned toward Ewan. "When we get to the topside, follow my lead. I need to figure out how to get out of this. I hope I can come up with a good story." Like how they traveled through time and showed up on Moira's dig. And how he'd get them all home safely. He looked up the ladder, and Miss White's rounded rear shifted in her tight khakis.

Ewan whispered back, "Aye, we need to figure out how to explain to Miss White how we appeared. Then how are we getting home to the future?"

Dominic handed Evie up the ladder. "When your head gets into the tunnel, it will be safe to open your eyes, Evie."

Once Evie was on the ladder, Dominic turned to Ewan. "I'm working on it. I just need to figure it out. Damn, I need more time."

Ewan started up the ladder and glanced over his shoulder. "Well, Uncle Dom, ye better hurry. I can see the light, and it's not far. Ye'll have some fancy explaining when we reach the top."

Chapter 3

Miami, Florida. The Museum of Science—Present Day

Bree stood shocked as Doug stammered again. "Th...the...they...I mean, it...Her, it was her, but not." Doug hiccupped and tried to draw in a breath, then hiccupped again.

Colin pinched the bridge of his nose and took a deep breath. "Doug, tell me again, but slowly, where are Evie, Ewan, and Uncle Dom?" So far, Colin had held his temper, but that pinch of his nose told Bree he'd nearly lost his patience.

Doug's blank look traveled from Colin to Brielle, then to his mother, Marie.

Doug breathed deeply when his younger sister, Kat, interrupted him. "Into the eye. They went in the eye."

Colin bent down to Kat and took her hand, grinning at her. "In the eye. Ye mean the big golden one on the wall?"

Kat nodded as Marie approached and kneeled next to Colin. "Kat, honey, are ye sure that's what ye saw? They went into the eye?"

Kat nodded, then turned to Bree. "But it's ye I have a message for." Bree walked between her husband and best friend and took Kat's hand, leading her away from the group.

Doug seemed to finally find his voice. "That's what I have been trying to tell ye. They went in the eye. They went to the white lady."

Colin and Marie glared at Doug as Marie spoke to her son. "What white lady?"

Doug pointed to the display with the life-sized picture of Moira White. "*The* White lady."

Bree sat on the edge of a display wall and took young Kat into her lap as Colin and Marie questioned Doug further.

Bree and Kat sat, whispering back and forth in a private moment. Bree wanted to make sure what she heard was what had really happened.

When finished, Bree finally pieced it all together. "Let me get this right, Kat, and tell me if I get anything wrong."

Kat nodded, wearing too serious an expression for a nine-year-old as she stared into Bree's face.

Bree smiled and took a deep breath. "You all came here because Evie wanted to see the eye."

Kat nodded.

"Then Uncle Dom made the mummy come alive, but not really, to trick you all."

Kat giggled and nodded.

Bree nodded back. Good so far. "Dom wanted to see the pretty lady, whom you call the White lady."

Kat nodded as Bree asked, "The one on the wall there?" She pointed to the picture of Moira White.

Kat nodded. "Uncle Dom said she was beautiful. I think he likes her."

Bree rubbed Kat's back. "Ah. You said Evie opened the eye to a movie?"

Kat nodded. "It was a movie about the pretty lady

she wanted to show Uncle Dom." Kat bowed her head. "That's when it happened."

Bree rubbed her back. "What happened, Kat? You can tell me. I promise no one is in trouble. We're just worried. Tell me."

Kat peered up at her as a tear escaped. "Evie couldn't control it. She said she lost her grip."

Bree wiped the tear away. "Lost her grip on what, Kat?"

Kat looked at the eye, then back at her. "The portal. She lost her grip on the portal in time."

Bree gasped. "A portal? You mean a portal in time?" *Oh God, the Fae and a portal. It's starting again.* The Fae had involved her children this time.

Bree glanced at Colin, then back at Kat. "Did Evie tell you this?"

Kat nodded slowly. "Evie told me in my head. She said to tell her ma she's sorry. She didn't mean to. The eye called her, so she had to come. She said she lost her grip. She's sorry." Bree grasped Kat's shoulders, her world nearly tilting on edge. A portal meant time travel.

"Where, Kat, or should I ask when?"

Kat sat up straighter. "Evie said not to forget that I had to get it right. 1930s, Egypt. They are with the White lady. That's what I am supposed to tell ye." Tell her? Evie sent Kat a mental message. Her heart beat hard—another power on top of the stone splitting!

Colin roared, "Brigid!" making everyone in the room jump. Must he do that now? The chapel wasn't real, and the Fae likely weren't in Florida, but back in Scotland.

Bree sat Kat beside her on the display wall and went to her husband. "Yelling for your Fae will not bring our kids back. We need to be smart about this."

Colin paced, panting. "It's the damned Fae. They are at it again." He stopped, tilted his head back, and roared again, "Brigid!"

A security guard entered from the hall leading to the Scottish display.

Marie crossed to him, speaking lowly.

Doug went to his sister and took her hand. "It'll be okay, Kat. We did our part by telling the truth."

After the security guard left, Marie returned to the group. "The reception ended without us. The museum is closed now. We must leave."

Bree gasped and went to Colin, who took her in his arms. Colin's gaze caught Marie's as he nodded to the exit. Bree stood with her ear to his chest, his heart hammering a hard beat.

Marie walked to Doug and Kat. "Kids, let's wait in the Scottish exhibit. I think Bree and Colin need some time alone before we go."

Marie put her arm around Doug, who held his sister Kat's hand, and they walked toward the hallway. "Will we still go get Da from the airport tonight?"

Marie nodded. "Aye, as soon as we leave here, we'll go there. Hopefully, his plane will be late, so he won't have to wait on us."

Kat sniffled. "Will Da be mad, mad at what happened?"

Marie shook her head, and her answer faded as they entered the hallway toward the Scottish exhibit.

Bree stood in Colin's arms as she turned and stared at the Eye of Ra. "I don't understand how she could open a portal by herself or send a message to Kat. I didn't think she had that much power."

Colin growled, "That damned sprite. She's playing with us again. By God, if anything has happened to the children."

Bree placed her finger on his lips. "There is nothing we can do until we hear from the Fae. Marie will pick up John from the airport. We'll regroup and plan."

As she removed her finger, Colin caught her hand, kissing the back. "Ye are the wise one today. Aye, John and I will plan how to go back and retrieve them."

She snorted. "You and John? You mean you and I."

Colin growled lowly as his finger pointed between them, much as he had in the past. "Ye and I will not be traveling in time. I will go back, and ye will wait here where ye are safe." Back to this conversation again. Oh, men!

Bree yanked her hand out of his grasp, stepping away. "They are my children as well as yours. We are better off as a team."

She stifled a sob at the thought of her children away from her. So far, she couldn't even call them.

Images of them as babies overwhelmed her as her eyes teared. "They are my babies, Colin. I have to go. What if something has happened to them?" Her throat closed as she spoke in a whispered sob. "What if one is hurt?"

Colin gathered her in his arms. "Brielle, they are with yer brother. Yer great American Air Force Special Ops, I-can-defeat-anything-and-fly-any-manufactured-craft brother. Hell, he can probably fly something not manufactured by man and has. He's just unable to tell anyone."

Bree sighed as Colin kissed the top of her head.

They both turned to the Eye of Ra as Colin spoke. "Dominic is with them. What can go wrong?"

****

Tanis, Egypt, 1939

Dominic poked his head out of the shaft to World War III. The tent encampment, as well as the dig site, were under attack. Local villagers fought against other villagers. Everyone's clothing looked the same: white tunics with pants and head wraps. Dominic couldn't tell who was on whose side. He glanced to the side as a tent flap opened with the breeze. He spied Ewan and Evie hidden inside. Evie huddled behind Ewan, who held a rifle with a bayonet. He'd have to make a run for it to get to them.

Jumping from the shaft, he crouched, assessing the area. Mapping his route, he ran for the tent. Two men shifted as they wrestled before him. One punched the other, and he fell to the ground. The other man went for another without even noticing that Dominic stood there. Dominic bent down and grabbed the fallen man's rifle and, at a run, made it to Evie and Ewan.

Entering the tent, he kneeled beside Ewan. "You know how to use that thing?"

Ewan nodded. "Aye. Da insisted we learn. Evie can shoot as well."

Dominic breathed, "Thank God." He peered from his hiding place and spied Moira fighting against a larger man who looked like a typical thug from a bad B-rated 1930s movie. The crazy woman would get herself hurt or, worse, killed. He had to help her. Ewan said he knew how to use the gun.

Decision made, he turned to Ewan. "Stay hidden

no matter what happens. I'm going to try to put a stop to this. Only shoot if you must, but try stabbing them with the end first. It's a knife."

Ewan nodded as Dominic ran out of the tent, heading to Moira. She kicked the large man in the shin while he held her arm. Along the way, Dominic picked a revolver off a fallen man.

He came up behind the large brute and whacked him on the head with the butt of the revolver. The thug swayed for a moment before dropping like a rock.

Once he fell, Moira's shocked expression met his. "Thanks, but I had it under control."

Dominic shoved the revolver in his belt and grabbed her arm. "Sure, you did. His shin took such a severe beating." Moira was beautiful but not wise. Women—a complication always.

She spoke rapidly as he pulled her along with him. "They aren't out to hurt anyone. They are only trying to steal my work." She sighed. "And make a mess of my site."

Dominic grunted as he stepped over a knocked-out man. "Sure, they are, with loaded guns. Not hurting anyone, just punching the crap out of everyone in the way." Were all women so blind to the dangers they were in? Hell, even the highly trained females on his team sometimes lost their heads in battle.

As he turned toward the twins' hiding place, another thug moved before them and punched Dominic. His instant reflexes kicked in, and he immediately hit him back.

The man reached for Moira. *Enough!* He needed to change the odds.

As Dominic shoved Moira behind him with his

elbow, he drew the revolver and pointed it in the man's face. He shifted the rifle in his hand, spun it in a circle, cocking the gun, and pointed it at the man at his side.

A loud voice boomed over the chaos in Arabic, spoken with a French accent. "*Waqef! kalakim tugvoa alaan.*" *Stop! All of you stop now.*

Everyone froze as Dominic held his gun to both thugs' faces while Moira stayed behind him. Thankful for the tour of duty in Saudi Arabia, Dominic understood the language, but he didn't hint that he did. He needed any edge he could gain.

The village men parted as a tall man in a pristine white suit sauntered toward Dominic. When he arrived, he waved the thugs away. They shrugged at Dominic and walked away.

Dominic shifted the revolver and the rifle to the Frenchman's face, the group's apparent leader. He cocked the handgun and stared down the barrel at the man, who seemed surprisingly relaxed. He appeared amused, which angered Dominic even more.

He spoke in English, the drawn French accent grating Dominic's nerves. "Moira, you have a new friend. Please introduce us."

Dominic spoke before giving Moira a chance to respond. "The question here isn't who I am but who you are."

The Frenchman leered. "Why, how rude of me. *Comme c'est maladroit*, how clumsy. Of course, introductions are in order."

He bowed as Dominic's guns followed him.

The fop rose, and Dominic held the rifle closer, touching the Frenchman's nose as he spoke. "I wouldn't make any more movements. My trigger finger is a little tight today, and I haven't shot anything in a while. Wouldn't want anything to go off—" Dominic smirked. "—by accident." God, he'd love nothing more than to shoot this fop, steady and calm—defense above all else.

The Frenchman swallowed and stood fully. "*Bonjour*, I am Pierre Lenoir, a close, personal friend of Miss White."

A huff came from behind Dom as her hands rested on his back.

His shoulders shifted at the charged contact as she hissed, "Don't trust him, and he's no friend." An overwhelming sense of protecting her filled Dominic.

Pierre chuckled. "Such as it is with old friends. Old jokes as well. And *qui êtes vous,* who are you, fine sir?"

Dominic caught a movement from the corner of his eye, shifted the revolver, and shot. The bullet landed in the dirt at the foot of a villager, sneaking away with an artifact in his hand.

He held the gun on the victim, then slowly cocked it again. "Next one of your boys who moves, I'll hit."

Moira gasped from behind him. "He has the Divine Family Statue. It's mine. I found it."

Dominic stared at the gold artifact in the man's hands. A woman was on one side, and it seemed like a sun rose above her head. Her hand held out to the center, where a smaller form sat atop a black pedestal. The thief's hands covered the other tall form.

A scuffle sounded to Dominic's left. Before he could react, another of Pierre's thugs dragged two people toward them. The jerk held the twins each from the back of their button-down shirts. Ewan repeatedly hit the man in the chest. Evie tried to reach behind her to grab the hand on her shirt. Their scuffle made a large dust cloud as they approached. When the thug stopped, Evie kicked him in the crotch and stood grinning. The brute stood firm with only a grunt.

Moira spoke from behind Dominic. "Oh God, he has the children." Damn it. Not the kids. Women and more complications. Why couldn't this be easy, and he just shot them all? But Dominic couldn't do that. While he had killed in defense, he was not a murderer.

Pierre smirked at Dominic as he stepped back. "More friends of yours, Moira. You seem to have so many new friends today." He grinned as he eyed Dominic, the expression more of a smirk. "Well, my new friend. It seems you hold hostage—something of value I want." He waved to the large man holding the kids. "And I have something of value you want. *D'un métier, a trade.*"

Pierre spoke harshly in Arabic. "Point a gun at the children."

A man beside the thug pointed a gun at Evie's head. He turned to stare at Dominic and smirked as he cocked it. Ah hell, now he'd done it. Dominic was truly becoming angry, but the situation called for calm.

As he took a deep breath, Moira cried out from behind and went around him, her arms out. "No, don't. Take the statue, but don't shoot the children. I'll give you the statue if the children can come to me. Just put down the guns, all of you."

She glanced over her shoulder at Dominic with a pleading look, then back at Pierre. "Children, come to me."

Maybe Moira gave them the edge they needed. Careless as the move was, he admired her courage. But

Dominic kept his guns pointed at his target, the leader. One foul move, and he'd take him out, then grab Moira and the kids, making a run for safety.

The thug with the gun beamed at Pierre, who raised an eyebrow when Dominic didn't lower his weapon. "Sir? The statue or the children. Which shall it be?" Backed into a corner and no way out without bloodshed. Dominic hated the odds but had to concede his position.

Dominic uncocked his revolver and lowered the rifle and the handgun, but he never took his gaze from Pierre. Pierre nodded to the brute, who dropped his weapon as the man with the statue approached Pierre, handing it to him.

The children ran to Moira, who hugged them to her.

She glared at Pierre as he spoke. "Seems I have another one of your finds, Miss White. You really should keep better track of your—artifacts." He turned and addressed the crowd in Arabic. "My men, leave this place."

His men quietly followed him away. Some helped the wounded to their cars beside the campsite. Dominic kept his eye on this Pierre guy. He didn't like the way he ogled Moira as he walked away. This wasn't over by a long shot. It seemed this Frenchman had just begun.

Moira rose and took the children in each arm. She backed up and stood by Dominic as her men tended to the wounded and tried to clean up the mess the attack had left in its wake.

Dominic stood rooted in his spot, observing Pierre and his men leaving. If only the odds had been different, but the kids' and Moira's safety was paramount. Pierre's men loaded in their cars and took off across the desert. The threat was gone, for now.

Ewan moved beside him. "I'm sorry, Uncle Dom."

Dominic shoved the revolver in his belt and tousled Ewan's hair. "It's okay. What's important is you both are safe. Did he hurt either of you?"

Both children shook their heads in perfect unison. He snorted. Twins.

Evie turned to Moira. "I'm sorry about yer statue, Miss White."

Moira grinned at Evie. "Call me Moira, and I'll get the statue back...somehow." She exhaled and glanced around. "Why don't you kids head to the cook's tent for water? It's over there." She pointed to the tent at the end of a line.

Both children peered at Dominic in near-perfect unison, who nodded his permission.

As the kids walked away, Dominic turned to her. "Are you okay?"

Moira sighed as she watched Pierre's group travel away from her campsite.

She turned to look at him. "Thank you. You saved the campsite from ruin. Saved my other artifacts."

Dominic leaned the rifle against the box of supplies. "Well, I didn't save the statue, but I did stop the attack." He looked at Pierre's group driving away in the distance, then back at Moira. "How often has he struck?" He stepped closer. "Has he hurt anyone?" Obviously, this wasn't the first time the Frenchman had attacked. And by the looks of it, it wouldn't be the last.

She breathed and ran a shaky hand over her hair. Unruly auburn wisps floated in the breeze like the entire mass tried to escape their confines. Her nerves seemed rattled, but she appeared unhurt.

After another deep breath, she spoke. "They usually aren't so heavily armed. Fortunately, he has only hurt my pride, reputation, dig, and stolen my finds."

Dominic smirked. "Is that all?"

She sniffled and gave him a wobbly grin. At least she had her humor, a sign this hadn't affected her deeply. Yet concern still rose in him. A woman left to defend herself with mere villagers as protection.

Moira sniffled and blinked. So, she was affected. She needed more help and protection.

Dominic stepped closer and rubbed his hand up and down her arm, trying to soothe her. "You should hire protection to guard you and your campsite." After speaking, he inhaled, and the faint scent of jasmine floated to him, sweet and light.

She sniffled. "I thought I had with Nubi and his villagers, but it seems even that is not enough anymore. Pierre grows bolder."

He exhaled. Mere villagers were not trained soldiers familiar with defense tactics. Did Moira even realize what she faced with a man like Pierre? One whose greed forced him to grow bolder in his pursuit of each thing he desired. Men like him were easy to read but hard to predict.

Dominic took her hand in his and held it in front of him. "For now, I am here and will protect you."

Dominic studied Moira. Her eyes were a deep hazel, like a dark emerald. She seemed so innocent and vulnerable after the attack on her site. He held her hand in his for a moment, caressing the fingers. The calluses from working with brushes contrasted the softer parts not used to hard labor. A long, wiry, reddish curl escaped her hair in the wind and blew across her face. Dominic couldn't resist himself. He reached for the ringlet and placed it behind her ear.

She glanced down as a blush spread across her face. "Thank you, Dom. I appreciate the help—while you are with us."

Dominic smiled. "Whatever you need, I'll be here." He studied the area—all clear. "Let's clean this mess up before nightfall."

She regarded the site. Her gaze shot back at Dominic, who let go of her hand. *Uh-oh.* Her eyes squinted as if she recalled why they came up from the burial chamber and how they got here. Damn, she was a fast thinker.

She placed her hands on her hips as she spoke. "Which brings me to my question. How did you three end up in the tomb? Before the attack, I asked Nubi if he saw you before you fell. He said no one approached the site. That was just before Pierre's cars came over the hill."

Dominic looked away and sighed.

She grumbled, "You aren't going to try and tell me some mysterious mummy dumped you in my dig site, are you? So how exactly did you end up in the tomb without ever entering it?"

Dominic glanced down, rubbed his neck, then peeked at her. "We're tourists, lost." Would she buy it? Likely not. She was a smart, educated woman who was not afraid of men she should be frightened of.

She huffed a laugh. "Lost tourists, I believe. But you still haven't answered my question. How did you get into the tomb?"

Dominic picked up the rifle and strode past her as he spoke over his shoulder. "You wouldn't believe me if I told you." Women, a complication he didn't need right now. He needed to figure out how to get himself and the kids home to the future.

As he passed her, Moira grabbed his arm. "I have spent my life in ancient tombs of Egypt. Curses, strange wind underground, stories of the dead becoming the undead. You'd be surprised at what I would believe."

Dominic inspected her face, trying to find any hint of mistrust or deceit. If he told her the truth, would she not only believe it but keep his secret, the Fae secret?

She rolled her eyes. "It can't be that bad. The locals claim the tomb we were in is cursed. But you three popping in is the first strange thing we've encountered here." She stepped closer. "Whatever the explanation, it will remain between us." He'd have to enlist her help. The damn portal sat in the middle of her dig site.

Dominic moved closer, peering directly into her emerald eyes. "I have your word on that. And if we need help, you will give it? Regardless of how strange it may sound?"

Moira nodded, stepping back and putting her hand out for a shake. Dominic eyed the hand, then her, and shook it but didn't let it go. *Hit her with it all. Shock her so she won't believe it.*

He pulled her closer and spoke low, ensuring only she heard. "We are from the future. The Eye of Ra is a portal between times and places. We came by accident and need to get home."

Moira glanced at their hands, then at his face. "Future, eh? A portal in time?" Still holding his hand, her other flipped her hair, which had fallen on her face. "Some story. I suppose you have good fighting skills for a man from the future." Was that flirting? Did he detect a challenge in her eyes?

Dominic beamed at her compliment. He knew he had mad skills. She did not know half of all he could do.

"Military training. You could say I have skills." He placed his foot behind hers and pulled her hand, flipping her to the ground as he landed on top of her. Moira let out a grunt at the impact. Dominic's face was just above hers, their breaths mingling. Dominic didn't know why he did it, but he felt an attraction to the woman, one he couldn't explain. Jasmine, the scent came from her neck, like a sweet perfume.

Moira smirked. "Is that the best you can do?"

He grinned. This woman had no idea. "Trust me, I can do a lot better. Do I have your word? Our secret is safe, and you'll help us get back through the portal?"

Moira chuckled. "A time portal? That is something I have never seen. You do know telling tall tales leads to nothing but lies?" He never lied outside of a mission, especially to a woman. Women, on the other hand, were well-known liars. But Moira was different.

Dominic shifted his hand to her face, caressing it. "I don't lie, and I don't tell tall tales. I always tell the truth."

Moira tilted her head. "The truth means you'll show me a portal in time. Something that doesn't exist." Smart and a challenge. He liked these odds much better.

Dominic shifted his face closer to hers as he whispered, "You'll help us, tall tale or not?"

Moira shrugged as his breath mingled with hers. "Yes, I'll help you." He didn't know why, but the overwhelming urge to kiss her flooded his senses.

Dominic nodded slowly. "May I seal our deal with a kiss?"

Moira smirked. "First, he demands I believe he's from the future. Now he wants to steal a kiss." God, she was beautiful, and that spark made her irresistible.

Dominic's head dropped closer to her face, their lips barely touching. "Not stealing, giving." He kissed her lightly.

She sighed into his mouth. Unable to stop himself, he deepened the kiss. She moaned, and he took advantage of her open mouth as his tongue plundered hers. She shifted in his embrace, and he regretfully ended the kiss.

Moira replied. "You, sir, have a deal."

Chapter 4

That night, Moira pulled a bottle from her bag and gave it to Dominic. He eyed the bottle, then her.

She shrugged. "It's some of my favorite gin. It's a good Egyptian blend."

At his raised eyebrow, she replied, "I keep it around for a sleeping aid."

Dominic laughed as he took the bottle and tipped it for a swig. He hummed and handed her back the bottle. After a typical campsite dinner of rice and beans, Evie, Ewan, and Dominic sat around her campfire. Moira and Dom passed the bottle between them. She took sips as the juniper berry flavor hit differently each time.

Moira glanced at the twins. Evie watched the fire. Ewan was almost asleep sitting up. She grinned at the typical teenagers.

Evie spoke as she stared at the flames. "Moira?" Moira sat up as Evie turned to her. "The statue they took. Was it important?"

Moira sighed. "Yes, it was. It was a great find." She grinned as she looked at the twins. She always wished for a sibling. The statue was such a revolutionary find. One that meant so much to her since it represented family.

"It was my favorite find, the statue of the Divine Family. It is one of the greatest Egyptian folk tales and explains why the pharaohs are revered."

Dominic shifted back and lounged on his elbow as he gazed at her.

She peeked at him and blushed. "It is my favorite story because it talks about family."

Evie grinned. "Will ye tell us the story? I haven't heard it before."

Moira stared into the flames. "I recall my uncle telling it. He told it so well, and his deep baritone voice always carried. He'd chew on his cigar, then wave it in the air, adding drama as he told the tale. I can almost smell the cigar now."

"The hope of the righteous is gladness; the expectation of the wicked perishes."

Evie hit Ewan, and Ewan sat up straighter as she mouthed something to him that Moira didn't quite catch. Kids.

Moira breathed. "My uncle told it better than I ever could, but I'll do my best."

"The pharaohs of Egypt traced the Divine Family's lineage to the God Horus. Horus was the son of Osiris and Isis, two of the nine primal Gods of the Egyptians." Moira glanced at Dominic, who had handed her the bottle, and she took a sip and handed it back. Dominic held on to the bottle, stopping Moira, who peered at him. He winked at her. She released the bottle and continued her story. From the corner of her eye, Moira caught Evie's smirk at their exchange.

"The Divine Family story begins when Osiris, the God of order, reigned on Earth as king and married Isis. When they shared Isis' magical healing powers and vast knowledge with the people, they taught the practice of government, religion, and marriage. They brought civilization and humanity to the land."

Dominic tilted the bottle back and took a healthy swig.

Ewan spoke from beside Evie. "Ewww, marriage and kissing? That's gross."

Dominic swallowed and grunted a laugh.

Moira pointed her finger at Ewan. "Love, marriage, and kissing are not such a bad thing, Ewan. One day, you may like it."

Evie snickered as Ewan rolled his eyes and settled into a more comfortable position.

Moira grinned, liking the teens' banter. While Nubi and his tribe treated her as family, she still missed her uncle—her family. Her gaze caught Dominic, who watched her with hooded eyes. Their kiss flashed in her memory. Did he find it as moving as she had?

She shook herself and returned to telling her tale. "Seth, the God of disorder, and Osiris' brother, held a banquet for the king. He invited his guests to lie down in a great coffin he had made for the king as a gift. When Osiris climbed in, Seth and his conspirators slammed and nailed down the lid. They'd weighed the coffin down with lead and cast it into the Nile, murdering his brother."

Ewan threw a twig into the fire. "What a jerk."

Moira nodded; Seth was awful. "The death of Osiris threw the cosmos into chaos, making the Gods weep. Isis, greatly distraught, wandered throughout the land searching for her husband. She found the casket and returned to Egypt with it. She hid the casket and herself from Seth in the delta marshes."

Dominic huffed, "Sure, nothing spooky about a woman hiding with her husband's body in the marshes. It sounds like most every horror movie made."

Ewan and Evie laughed, but Moira glared at him in confusion. She hadn't seen many movies but had heard about them.

She turned to Dominic. "Horror. What is a horror movie?"

Ewan spoke as Dominic's gaze shot to him. "Horror, ye know all blood and gore."

Dominic cleared his throat as he shook his head at Ewan, who sat back and grumbled.

Strange, most movies she knew of were happy. But one with blood and gore, she'd never heard of.

Dominic smiled. "We interrupted. Continue, please."

Moira shrugged and continued her story as he grinned at her. "Isis anointed Osiris' body with precious oils and restored Osiris to eternal life as King of the Dead. While grieving over her husband's body, she transformed into a kite. As she flew over the body, she conceived a child. Together, they became the Divine Family."

Ewan blew a laugh. "That's not how it really works. To make a baby, he has to…"

Dominic spoke swiftly. "Enough, Ewan."

Evie stifled a laugh as Dominic glared at both teens. Moira thought it was sweet that Dominic looked out for the teens. While her uncle was nice and caring, he hadn't watched over her education closely and how she'd found out about sex. Well, walking in on a couple wasn't a great way to find out how it all worked, but oh well.

When they settled, Moira spoke again. "Isis tried to hide her pregnancy and stayed in the marshes where she gave birth to her son, Horus. Isis hid the child in the swamps. One day, she left her son to search for food, and upon her return, she found him half dead. Seth had found them, entered the marsh, transformed into a poisonous snake, and bit the child."

Evie shivered. "I don't like this Seth guy."

Moira nodded. "Many didn't and don't to this day."

Dominic handed her the bottle, but she shook her head and drank water from a cup, needing to keep her head about her. Dominic was attractive, and the earlier kiss echoed in her mind. Sitting by the fire, sharing a story, drinking gin, she could easily get lost in his company.

She sat up and shook herself. "When Horus fell ill, the Earth fell into darkness. The High Gods assured Isis that the Earth would remain in darkness, that wells would dry up, and that all crops would fail. They claimed evil would triumph over good until she cured Horus. Then, in the sun's name and the powers of Ra, the high gods exorcised the poison from Horus' body and healed the child.

"The people of the marshland rejoiced with Isis at her son's recovery. Horus became the model of the pharaohs, the sun God's representative on Earth. The Gods claimed it was now the duty of the people to protect the pharaohs from harm and to love and respect them. If they did not, world order would collapse, and the people would perish." Moira took another sip of water.

"When Horus was a young man, he and his uncle Seth quarreled over who was the legitimate, divinely appointed ruler of Egypt. They held a tribunal of the Gods to settle the dispute over who would rule.

"But those who have hope will renew their strength. They will run and not grow weary; they will walk and not be faint; they will soar like wings on eagles."

Evie gasped, then covered her mouth. Ewan eyed her. Moira saw their exchange. What were the twins up to? They both turned in unison, staring at her with an identical expression. It must be a twin thing.

"The Gods made Horus king of the Lands of Egypt, and Seth took on the role of defender of Ra. Horus became the God of kingship, and the pharaohs traced their lineage to him. The God who triumphed over evil. Horus received the Eye of Ra—the supreme power of the creator—and passed it on to all the pharaohs through the ages."

Evie tilted her head. "So, the Eye of Ra, the eye in the tomb. It's powerful?"

Moira peered at Evie. "The eye is gold, but the symbol is powerful."

Evie glanced at Dominic, who shook his head at Evie. What was that?

Dominic sat up. "Well, kids, story time is over. Time to tuck you in. I'll walk you to your tent."

Ewan sat up. "But, Uncle Dom, it's not a school night."

Moira hid her smile as Dominic glared at the twins.

Ewan sighed. "Fine! Evie, come on." Both kids rose and walked away.

He handed Moira the bottle. "Keep it warm for me. I'll be right back." He rose and winked at her.

****

Moira sat gazing into the fire as she held the gin bottle. Dominic's kiss was fresh in her mind. She reached up and touched her lips. Her first romantic kiss from a man, and her lips still tingled.

Dominic approached, and she quickly moved her hand away. She handed him the gin bottle. He accepted it and eased down beside her, his hip touching hers.

She nudged him with her shoulder. "So, Dom, got the kids to bed?"

Dominic sipped from the bottle. "Yes. I hope they get some sleep after this exciting day."

Moira chuckled. "I suspect they will be up half the night."

Dominic huffed. "I hope not." He looked over at Moira, who kept her head down. "I am worried about you, about what you will do after we leave tomorrow." Was that concern she heard in his voice?

Moira glimpsed at Dominic, then away. "Oh, I suppose I will keep digging like I always do."

Dominic snorted. "That is not what I meant, and I think you know it." Overbearing men. She'd had enough of them in her life.

Moira heaved a heavy sigh. "Dom, I will deal with Pierre as I always have. I'll regroup and file my findings sooner so he cannot take them so easily."

Dominic set aside the bottle and turned to face Moira. "He will not make it any easier. You say he grows bolder with each attack. When will you take this seriously and hire protection to keep you safe?"

"I have Nubi and the villagers to keep me safe. You should not worry, a military man from a supposed future. Remember, you leave tomorrow." She exhaled. "None of this will be your concern."

Dominic reached out and took her hand in his. "It is my concern. What if you went missing? Mysteriously missing or something."

Moira glanced at their clasped hands, then at Dominic's face. He seemed so earnest. Could he be trying to tell her something, something of the future? She shook her head. Fanciful thinking. As he said, he couldn't be from the future—only lost tourists.

She rose, but Dominic grabbed her shoulders. "Please promise me you'll hire extra help."

Moira stopped and stared into his eyes, so caring. She could get lost in the light blue, the same shade as a bright, clear sky. She recalled their first glimpse in the tomb earlier in the day, and the Earth seemed like it stopped. Dominic leaned close and brushed her cheek with his hand. The scent of light musk came off him mixed with sweat, not offending but alluring.

He stopped as their mouths almost touched. "So sweet."

He kissed her. His lips, softly at first, lightly brushed hers in an invitation to open her mouth. She closed her eyes and could not resist. She opened her mouth to his kiss, already familiar to her.

Dominic growled in response and deepened the kiss, tilting her head to the side. His tongue danced with hers as he gathered her in his arms, sliding her across his lap so she sat perfectly in his embrace.

He slowly ended the kiss. "God, Moira, the things you do to me." He kissed her lips quickly. "What I wouldn't give to stay here."

He was a good-looking man interested in her, a woman bent on digging up the dead for a living focused on discovering the past of Egypt. Men weren't interested in her. Hell, her first kiss was earlier today. What was he really after?

Moira pushed against his chest. "Where are you really from, Dom?"

She tried to scramble out of his arms, but he held her tight against him. "It's as I told you. God, I knew you wouldn't believe me."

She pushed against him, and this time, he released her.

She scrambled, stomped away, then stopped and rounded on him from across the fire. "You drop into my dig, then Pierre attacks."

She turned a full circle, slapping her hand to her head. How could she be so stupid, so naïve? One kiss was all it took.

So distracted, she kissed the very man who brought her enemy to rob her—again. "You're with Pierre, that's it. That's why you seduce me."

Dominic stood so fast that sand flew off his body. "I am not with that asshole! I *saved* you."

Moira fisted her hands at her sides, wanting to strike him. "Ha, you distracted me! And Pierre got away with the Divine Family Statue. You distract me now." She waved her hand. "Well, I won't have it. Tomorrow, you leave, and I will keep my artifacts and continue my dig."

She stormed off, calling over her shoulder, "I have one of Nubi's villagers watching you. So if you try to steal anything, they will stop you."

****

He called after her, "Yeah, well, don't worry. I don't want any of your old crap."

Dominic watched the attractive Moira stomp off, her rear moving enticingly in her pants. Damn, she was beautiful. He ran his hand through his hair and sat by the fire.

Dominic spied the gin bottle, picked it up, and drew a hardy sip. "Women. They are just as infuriating in the past as in the future."

****

Later that night, Evie sat awake as the story rolled through her mind. Uncle Dom stumbled in a short while ago. Now, his light snores filled the tent.

She had a feeling about the statue. The significance of the artifact would not leave her. She kept seeing it in her mind's eye, and she felt maybe Brigid tried to tell her something but was too far away to communicate. They could do that at Dunstaffnage. Speak in their minds, but when she was away, there was nothing. There was something special about the statue, and she needed to figure out what that was.

Evie leaned close to her brother, whispering, "Ewan!"

Uncle Dom shifted but resumed his light snoring.

"Ewan. Are ye awake?" Evie whispered louder. "Ewan, are ye sleeping?"

Ewan shifted in his sleeping bag. "I was."

Evie sat up. "Ewan, the story. The one Moira told."

Ewan exhaled. "Aye, I know it was like the Stone of Hope Fae fable story."

Evie gaped at him. "The quote… 'But those who have hope will renew their strength. They will run and not grow weary; they will walk and not be faint; they will soar like wings on eagles.' "

It was from The Stone of Hope Fae fable and Moira's Divine Family story. Brigid had her and Ewan read the Fae book secretly, saying she wanted to give this generation a fair shot at defeating the evil Fae.

At first, she and her brother found reading the stories fun. But when it came time to read them repeatedly, it was a chore. Now Evie found relief that Brigid was stern in her lessons, forcing them to memorize each story.

Evie hugged her knees as the ramifications of Moira's story matching a Fae fable swirled in her head. "Ye know what that means."

Ewan snuggled into his sleeping bag. "Nothing. We go home tomorrow. So, Moira's story means nothing."

Evie sighed as the image of a green rectangular stone broken in half, like her parents' stone, flashed in the portal scene. "The Stone of Hope is here, Ewan. I saw it before I lost control of the portal. I saw it broken into two pieces. Green long rectangle, nearly two halves."

Ewan turned to stare at her. "Is that how ye lost control? Ye lost focus?"

Evie nodded. "Aye, but I think the stone caused me to lose focus. I think it wanted us to be here, to find it."

Ewan sat up. "Wait, can ye still do that trick where ye break apart a stone and put it back together again, whole?"

Evie nodded as the memory of Brigid showing her the rock meld came to her. "The first trick Brigid ever taught me when we were young. Aye, I can."

Ewan glared at the tent wall. "Well, then maybe the Fae did want us to be here."

A growl emitted from Uncle Dom's sleeping bag. "What you want to do is *sleep*. So, the others in the tent can get some rest."

Evie and Ewan startled, then settled into their

sleeping bags. They lay there in silence momentarily as Evie ran the day's events back through her mind. Moira mentioned the symbol of the Eye of Ra held power. That's likely how it became a time portal between realms. Brigid explained to her and her brother how there were different portals for different purposes. But the chapel door was a time portal and a pathway between the realms of Fae and humans. Other time portals existed, but Brigid never told them where they were.

Evie spoke softly to her uncle, "The eye has power, Uncle Dom. That's how I could open the portal so easily."

Uncle Dominic glanced back over his shoulder. "Yes, I surmised that as well. I told Moira we were from the future, but I doubt she believed me." He breathed. "Moira said she'd help, so she'll have to see the eye working. We can do nothing about that."

Ewan spoke softly, "But once we are through, what happens here? What will happen to Moira?"

Her uncle moved in his sleeping bag. The rustling sounded loud in the night. "She already mentioned a curse. I suppose she will consider it part of the curse of the mummy buried in the chamber. So, when we disappear, she'll think that." He hummed, then snorted.

Evie turned toward him. His hands rested under his head as he glowered at the tent ceiling.

"Ye like her, don't ye, Uncle Dom?"

He rolled over, facing away from her. "What I like doesn't matter. Getting us all home safe is what we focus on now." He turned slightly, his eyes and teeth glowing in the dark. "Get some sleep. Tomorrow, we go back home."

After a moment of silence, Uncle Dom's voice came to her. "Evie, can you break a stone in half and put it back together whole again?"

Evie shifted. "Aye, Uncle Dom."

He chuckled. "Any stone?"

"Well, I've only tried it on an Iona stone, but I bet any rock is the same."

"Amazing." He turned over. "Go to sleep."

Chapter 5

Colin strode away from Bree as she still spoke. He would not argue with her anymore. They'd arrived at the museum early this morning, an arrangement Bree made claiming they needed to adjust her Scottish display. In reality, they were there to travel back in time. Bree kept Colin up all night arguing about going with him to retrieve their kids. Colin growled because she still hadn't stopped.

Bree followed him close behind, her pleading voice pulling his heartstrings. "Colin, I have to go with you. They are our children."

Colin stopped, turned, and slashed his hand out. "No, Bree."

She pulled up before running into him.

He ran his hand through his hair and scowled at his wife, the mother of his kids and his true love. She could argue with the best solicitors in the law firm. Likely because she'd honed her skills debating with him. He needed to make her understand the risk she placed herself in. It would be hard enough to track down the twins and get them back. But to have her along to look after, to keep safe. He still debated with himself if he could keep everyone he valued from harm.

She stared back, tears in her eyes, and his heart nearly melted.

He stepped forward, took her face in his hands, and spoke softly. "I lost ye once in the portals. I can't do that again." The memory of her abduction at the hands of her ex-boyfriend who was possessed by Balor, the king of the evil Fae, still rocked his core.

He kissed her briefly and hard. She needed to know he did this for her. He didn't mean to hurt her, only to keep her protected.

A tear escaped her eye and trailed down her cheek. "It was I who lost you and had to bring you back. I can't lose the kids. I miss them already."

Colin wiped the tear away. "And ye will have them back soon. Once John and I retrieve them while ye wait here with Marie, safe."

He kissed her again and turned to John MacArthur, the captain of Dunstaffnage Castle and his dear friend.

John stood staring at the Eye of Ra. "Another portal, a portal in time?" Marie, his wife, stood next to him. Their children, Doug and Kat, were back at the hotel with a hired sitter. They wouldn't take any more chances with the kids near a Fae portal.

Colin moved and stood next to John, eyeing the gold monstrosity. "That's what the kids said. Evie opened it. Dom, Ewan, and she got sucked in."

Bree came to Colin's side, took his hand in hers, and leaned against him. "I still can't believe Evie opened a portal alone." His daughter, with Fae powers, was now strong enough to open a portal without help from a poem or the Fae. What was his world coming to, and where in the hell would this all end?

Bree turned and examined the room. He knew whom she searched for.

Marie followed her gaze.

Colin grunted. "Ye can look all ye want, Bree. Those damned Fae sisters won't show. They never show when I need them."

John huffed a laugh. "No *Fae Fable Book* to guide us. No help from the Fae." He peered at Colin. "So, how are ye going to open the portal?"

Colin growled. "Sheer will alone. I want my children back, safe."

Colin stood there staring at the Eye of Ra, willing it to open. Praying with all his might that he would blink, and Evie and Ewan would appear—nothing. He concentrated harder—the Fae, the damned duty to the stones. It was supposed only to be him affected. He gripped his wife's hand, willing the kids to him.

Bree's sniffle came to him. God, he could almost feel them in his arms—their children. He focused on the eye harder, and the damn thing hadn't changed. He growled again, dropping his wife's hand and made for the hallway leading out of the Egyptian display and into the Scottish display.

Tinkling laughter filled the room. "Giving up so easily, Colin? As my father said, that temper will be yer undoing one day."

Colin drew up and turned, glancing around the room. Empty.

Bree gasped and turned a full circle, as did Marie and John.

Colin roared, "Show yerself, ye damned sprite."

The tinkling laughter filled the room again. In a flutter of light, Brigid, Colin's Fae, appeared, sitting on the top of the Eye of Ra.

Bree took a step toward her.

Colin rushed forward, placing himself between

Bree and Brigid as Bree spoke. "Brigid, Colin and I want to go get the kids. Can you help us?"

Colin spoke over Bree, "John and I will go back in time to get the kids. Bree and Marie will stay here."

Brigid smirked. "Seems ye and yer true love cannot agree. And ye haven't even read the Fae fable story yet."

A shattering crystal sound filled the room as Morrigan appeared sitting on the mummy display with the *Fae Fable Book* in her lap. John and Marie gasped. Good, now the sisters were here with the damn book. Colin could get to the bottom of this mess and get his kids back.

John pointed at Morrigan. "She has the *Fae Fable Book*." He huffed. "Damn it! That means we'll have to go after another stone."

Morrigan peeked at John with an all too innocent look on her face. "Oh, not ye, John." She surveyed the room. "As a matter of fact, none of ye are in the plan to find the stone."

Colin stepped toward Morrigan. "Damn ye, the duty is mine. Ye'll not involve the children."

Morrigan shifted her focus to Colin. "It's too late, Colin. They already are involved."

Bree placed her hands on Colin's back and rested her head against him. "Oh, God, please tell me they are safe. Please tell me the kids are okay."

It was Brigid who responded. "Brielle, ye really should give yer children more credit. Gifted, they both are. Strong and wise."

Colin yelled at Brigid, "Answer her, ye wee waif! Ease a mother's fears! Are they safe?"

Brigid floated, sitting on Colin's shoulder as she

gazed at Bree. "Both are safe. Well cared for, and with yer brother."

Bree placed her arms around Colin, who reached around, pulling her into his arms as Brigid floated above them.

John pulled Marie into his arms as he spoke. "Colin, let's hear the Fae fable story. Maybe it will make sense once we know what we are in for."

Colin barked a laugh. "The story will not make sense, like all the ones before. I will still have to go back in time to get my kids."

Morrigan cleared her throat and flipped the pages of the *Fae Fable Book* as Brigid flew, settling next to her. "Oh, the Stone of Hope. I do like this one."

Bree gasped. "It's blue, diamond shaped." She glanced at Colin. "I've seen it. Your sister found it when we were…" She stopped mid-sentence, and Colin stared at his wife as many emotions crossed her face, one after another. He knew what she remembered, and it broke his heart.

She recalled the time when Balor possessed her ex and kidnapped her. He took her to the Viking times, the twelfth century. Colin didn't want her to relive her abuse at his hands, and she must have thought of the stone first before all the memories came rushing back. He loved and hated thinking of his sister Ainslie, who fell in love with a Viking man, Rannick Mac Raghnaill, only to choose to stay in the twelfth century to live with her true love.

He took Bree's hand in his and led her to the side of a display.

He sat her in his lap and held her like he always had, with all the love in his heart. "Ye'll not need to think of those times, Bree. Please clear yer mind. It was the Stone of Faith ye found, then lost, not Hope." He held her as she took a deep breath and then another.

John and Marie joined them, sitting on the edge of the half wall. Now, all sat ready to hear the next Fae fable story and learn what fate had in store for them.

Morrigan cleared her throat again as she read from the *Fae Fable Book*. "With the loss of the Stone of Hope, the human and Fae realms fell into a time of darkness, and evil ruled. The people of both realms waged wars, suffered casualties, and destroyed the land's bounty. In this time of death and destruction, the son born grew into a man. His father and uncle were old and near their end. He set out and sought the Stone of Hope. He felt if he could restore the Stone of Hope, he could mend the rift between brothers. By healing his family, he would heal both the Human and Fae realms."

Brigid sighed. "Morrigan, ye started in the middle of the story. They must know about the brothers before we get to the son traveling the world."

Colin growled, "Whatever it is, get on with it so I can get my children."

Brigid glanced at Colin. "Always so angry. My father was right. The evil Fae will use it against ye."

Morrigan turned the *Fae Fable Book* pages, but Brigid stopped her. "I'll tell an abbreviated version for the *annoyed boy* over here."

Colin huffed as Bree laid her head on his shoulders, rubbing his back. "Let her tell it, Colin. There may be some tidbit of info we need."

Brigid smiled at Bree. "Ye know, ye aren't the first to protect the stones. At one time, the Fae had the Stones of Iona protected separately. Back then, Da handpicked families to protect the stones of Hope, Faith, and Love. Losing the Stone of Hope brought despair to both the Fae and human realms, thus making the Fae realize they must keep the stones together. Apart, the stones are strong. But together, they are powerful. The brothers' father entrusted his two sons to protect the Stone of Hope for the Fae on his deathbed. The older brother kept the long rectangular green stone in a necklace and wore it constantly to remind the younger he held power."

Bree sat up. "The Lady Katherine MacDougall kept the Stone of Love in a necklace and buried it with her."

Brigid nodded. "Aye, that's how we protected the stones back then. We hid them in a necklace. At the beginning of MacDougall's guardianship, a true love protected the Stone of Love. Well, up until Katherine MacDougall."

Morrigan tsked. "Aye, that's a sad tale."

Brigid sat up taller as she continued. "But the brothers argued constantly over ownership of their land. Each of their pregnant wives went into labor. While waiting, the brothers got drunk and argued fiercely."

Morrigan picked up the story. "An evil Fae saw the argument and took advantage of the situation. He jumped the veil of time and challenged the brothers to a duel over the land, promising the winner the land. Something he could not deliver but had fun at the brothers' expense."

Brigid waved her hand. "It was the duel that broke the Stone of Hope. The younger brother cracked it, trying to stab the older brother."

Morrigan nodded. "With the Stone of Hope broken,

the evil Fae took the pieces, thus gaining control and ruling. It was a dark time."

Marie sat forward. "What of the wives and the births?"

Morrigan peered at Marie as she set the book down. "The younger brother lost his son. The older brother had a healthy son. In his jealousy, the younger brother vowed to get revenge upon the older brother."

Colin grumbled, "Is it just me, or are these damned fables getting longer with each one we encounter? Get to the part on Egypt and what this has to do with my children."

Morrigan picked up the book and read aloud. "The son, now a man, searched the earth for the Stone of Hope pieces as his father and uncle lay dying. He hoped to restore their relationship and help them find peace, as they had argued his entire life. Every place he could, he searched to find the stone halves."

Morrigan took a deep breath. "One day, he encountered an ugly crone begging for food in Egypt. Being a caring and giving man, he shared his food with her. She asked about his plight. He shared his tale with her, and she listened. Once done with his sad tale, she handed him a small Eye of Ra and told him if his heart was true, he could look into the eye, see his destiny, and fate would reward him."

John spoke softly, "The Eye of Ra."

They all turned to the eye as Morrigan's voice echoed in the room. "The man took the small symbol, doubtful of the outcome. How could an old woman know what his destiny held? But he stared into the eye and hoped against all hope. He prayed in his heart and soul for a way to help his father and uncle, the brothers, mend their hearts before death took them."

Her voice turned lighter. "Through the eye, he saw the old lady morph into a young, beautiful woman holding the long rectangular green Stone of Hope. Shocked, he shifted his eyes, and before him was the same young lady holding the green stone as it glowed. His heart beat in his chest for he had found the Stone of Hope and his true love."

Colin growled, "I am staring at the damn eye, and I see nothing."

Brigid quipped from her seat, "And ye will continue to see nothing till ye open yer heart and mind to the fable."

Bree whispered in Colin's ear, "Patience, my love. They will get to the important part soon." She sighed. "I hope."

Morrigan's voice rose, filling the room. "Together, the son and the woman returned to the son's home. Both brothers lay near death. Now faced with their misdeeds toward each other, they admitted their mistakes. The following morning, both brothers died, and the realms of human and Fae rose into the care of the good Fae as the recovery of the Stone of Hope banished the evil Fae."

Brigid spoke softly, "Colin, ye must remember. But those who have hope will renew their strength. They will run and not grow weary; they will walk and not be faint; they will soar like wings on eagles."

Colin shoved Bree aside, jumped up, and strode to Brigid, yelling at her, "That's it? Two petty brothers and a broken stone! A quote: to fly on eagle wings? How the hell am I supposed to bring my kids back from Egypt on that, and especially Egypt in the 1930s?"

Bree followed, grabbing Colin's arm. "Colin, maybe it is a metaphor. We must stop and think."

A wind filled the room in a swirling mass.

The center of the eye spun quickly.

Morrigan glanced at Brigid, who shrugged at her sister. "It's not me."

Morrigan peeked at the Eye of Ra. "It's not me either. Someone else is opening the portal—from the other side."

Colin moved around the mummy's sarcophagus as Bree held his hand and stood in front of the eye.

Brigid called over the wind, "Colin, this isn't good."

Releasing Bree's hand, he took another step closer to the golden artifact. "Good or not, I will get my kids back." The center spun fast. The eye opened in a swirl of smoke, and Evie stood before him, holding her hands out.

Bree cried out. "Evie." She ran toward the eye.

Colin grabbed her by the waist, stopping her. "Bree! I will go back! Ye stay here!"

As Evie called from the other side of the portal, they froze in each other's arms. "Ma! Da, I see ye!"

Morrigan raised her arms toward the Eye of Ra as Brigid called out over the wind. "No, Morrigan! Ye can't call the kids back! They must stay there!"

In a flash of light, the eye sucked Colin and Bree into the portal.

****

The portal closed. The wind stopped, leaving the room in silence.

Morrigan turned to Brigid. "It was a good Fae. There was a good Fae with Evie on the other side."

Chapter 6

Tanis, Egypt, 1939

Evie stood before the Eye of Ra. She had to open the portal so she, her brother, and her uncle could return to the future. It was up to her to fix this mess. She had to get them home. She raised her hands again and concentrated harder—*hope*. A wind blew through the underground tomb as the center of the eye spun.

Moira gasped as Dominic spoke. "That's my girl, Evie. Get us home."

Evie tried harder not to break her focus but sensed a presence at her side. She turned to her right, and a young male stood beside her, his arms outstretched toward the eye. She almost lost complete focus. He was tall with light, nearly white hair and had a boyish, good-looking face. When the wind whipped by, his hair flew out, and the tips of his ears were pointed. He looked like a model dressed in all white, like Brigid. When she peeked again, he winked at her. She focused on her task. She had to get the portal open.

She heard the boy in her head. *~Don't worry, Evie, I've come to help. Have hope. ~*

The portal opened, and she saw her parents standing on the other side.

Evie cried out. "Ma! Da, I see ye!" A shaft of pure white light shot out of the center of the Eye of Ra, hitting close to Evie's feet.

Margaret Izard

The boy next to her spoke in her head again. *~Oh, crap. Concentrate, Evie. ~*

Another shaft of light shot out, striking the sarcophagus, making the lid fly off, exposing the mummy inside. Another light hit the corpse.

Evie screamed. The portal closed, and the entire room was silent. Dizzy from the effort, blackness closed in on her vision.

****

Moira stood in awe. Evie had opened a portal in the center of the Eye of Ra. She took a deep breath and released it, then took another. She turned to Dominic, who stood staring at her with a tilt to his smile, then raised an eyebrow. Moira rolled her eyes and rushed forward, arriving by Evie's side simultaneously with her brother Ewan.

A groan came from the back of the sarcophagus. "Damn it, Bree, I told ye to stay behind." A Scotsman growled from behind the casket.

Ewan jumped up and ran around the coffin. "Ma, Da, ye're here!"

Dominic groaned. "Shit."

Moira squinted at him as she tried to revive Evie. A man and woman came from behind the coffin with Ewan.

The woman cried out when she saw Evie. "Is she hurt?" She ran to them.

Moira glimpsed up. "No, I think she just fainted." The beautiful woman kneeled beside Evie, patting Evie's face. "Evie baby, Mommy's here. It's all right, dear."

Moira peered at Evie and then at the woman, seeing the resemblance. "I'm Moira."

The woman peeked up. "I'm Bree."

From across the room, Dominic grumbled, "I'm screwed."

Moira glared at him and frowned.

Wait, the woman called herself mommy. "You're her mother? That means Dom is your brother, right?"

Bree nodded as she held Evie's head in her lap.

Moira studied the woman before her. She was dressed in slacks and a blouse, which were not much different from the clothes she owned. "He said you were from the future."

Bree nodded again and glanced at Dominic, who stood glaring at them.

Evie came around slowly and sat up with her mom's help. "Did ye see the boy? The one in white?"

Bree stared at her with an eyebrow raised. "A boy?"

Moira shook her head at Bree's silent inquiry.

Bree sat with Evie. "Let's let you rest a bit." She helped rest her daughter against the coffin's base.

Colin strode to Dominic as Ewan marched behind his father at the same gait.

Dominic stood rubbing his neck. He peeked up at Colin, who stood there glaring at him.

Moira rose as Colin glared at Dominic, who placed his hands on his hips and glared back. Both men possessed a formidable energy yet appeared to have a familiar friendship. "Brothers in arms" rang through Moira's mind.

Colin was the first to break the silence. "Well, they seem to be well. But ye are in big trouble, brother-in-law." Family, they were all family. The realization made Moira smile—Dominic's family.

Dominic pointed his finger first at Ewan, then Evie, and back at Colin again. "Th-they are *your* children. *Teenagers* with Fae powers."

Colin folded his arms across his chest. "Aye, they are that."

Ewan folded his arms just like his da. "Aye."

Colin pointed his finger at his son. "Ye are in even bigger trouble. Ye were supposed to care for yer sister, not let her time travel."

Ewan threw his arms wide. "Me? It's her fault."

Bree rose, crossing to Colin. "Now, Colin, let's not get hasty."

There was a loud scuffle, and Moira turned. Pierre Lenoir held Evie in his arms. His hand was over her mouth, and the other had a revolver at her temple.

Oh, God, not Pierre again! "Evie!"

Pierre cocked the gun, and everyone in the tomb turned his way and froze. "*Ne bougez pas. No one moves.* I'll be taking the girl. The one with the powers."

He backed up to the ladder, the only entrance or exit to the tomb. Pierre pulled her with him as Evie whimpered.

Moira, being closer, made a move toward Pierre. "Pierre, please, she's only a child."

Colin growled behind Moira.

Pierre shifted Evie in his arms as his eyes went wide, almost wild. "Moira, she has powers. You saw them. I saw them." Not the children. Desperate for anything to release Evie, Moira offered all she had.

Moira held her hands out in front of her. "Pierre, you can have it, the whole dig. All yours. Just release the girl."

His bitter laugh filled the small chamber. "Of all

the treasures you have found, Moira, this, by far, is the best one. And I shall steal another from you again!" *But Evie wasn't hers!*

Moira's gaze went to Evie, who stared back with pleading eyes. God, of all the things Pierre could steal, a child. She had to do something, but what?

Bree spoke behind her, a sob caught in her voice. "Colin, do something. H-he's taking my baby."

Colin growled, "I can't. He'll shoot her before I can get halfway across the room."

Bree cried out, "Dom, help, please."

Dominic grunted but stood frozen. Pierre could still shoot them from the ladder.

Moira looked around the room, trying to see if there was anything she could use or do.

A moaning groan filled the chamber. "Mmmmmmmmmm."

Pierre turned to Moira, and his eyes shifted to something behind her. "*Merde!*" *Shit.*

She turned around. A hand rose from inside the casket. She gasped, and everyone turned to the sarcophagus. A groaning came again as the hand grasped the casket's side, and the dead body sat up.

Ewan stepped closer to his da. "Uncle Dom, please tell me that's ye playing another trick on us."

Dominic glanced at Moira and then back at the mummy. "Ewan, I wish to God that was me, but it's not."

Pierre shouted, "Get up the ladder, girl, hurry! And no tricks. I have a gun."

Colin made a move toward Pierre, who turned the gun on him. "No, monsieur. You will remain still, or I'll shoot her from here."

Clearing the casket, the wrapped pharaoh stood staring at Bree, who backed up slowly.

Dominic turned to Moira. "You said the mummy is cursed. What curse?" *Well, this is a first.* She'd encountered air blowing through a chamber and falling sand. But a living dead mummy?

Moira shrugged. "Well, all pharaoh tombs are cursed."

The mummy grabbed Bree, who screamed.

Dominic lounged for the pharaoh as he pulled Bree toward the Eye of Ra. "The curse, Moira. What is the curse?"

Moira sputtered, "A pharaoh's curse is the same in all tombs. If you disturb the dead, bad luck, illness, or death shall come to you."

Dominic punched the corpse, who roared in his face, then turned, kissing Bree.

She sputtered and spat. "Eww, it kissed me. Why?"

Moira gasped. *This burial is Psusennes I. He's a pharaoh. The tomb is marked wrong.* She was right. This dig was valuable.

She turned to Bree. "He—he thinks you are his wife. He married his sister Mutnedjmet. I believe she's buried in the tomb next to this one." Moira glanced up, catching Bree's eyes. "He thinks you're her."

Dominic punched the wrapped body again, who picked up Bree and dumped her into the casket.

The mummy grabbed a blade resting near the casket and swung it at Dominic, who ducked calling out, "Colin, I could use some help here."

A gunshot rang through the chamber.

Moira's gaze shot to the ladder as Colin ducked from the shaft opening. "I'm a little busy trying to save my daughter."

Ewan crawled, hiding under the sarcophagus. He reached out, grabbing the pharaoh's leg and tripping him. The mummy fell, dropped the blade, and roared in Ewan's face. Who opened his mouth wide and roared back.

Dominic grabbed the blade and hacked the corpse. "The curse for this asshole, Moira." He spoke each word with a slash. *Whack!* "What." *Whack!* "Is." *Whack!* "It?" Dominic swung the knife as he said the last, and the mummy kept rolling away, forcing Dominic to miss each time.

Moira helped Bree out of the sarcophagus.

Ewan crawled out from under the casket and stood with Bree and Moira as they huddled between the coffin and the Eye of Ra.

"It won't help you defeat him. It's the same as the Divine Family. The hope of the righteous is gladness; the expectation of the wicked perishes."

Bree gasped. "That's a quote from the Fae fable story, the Stone of Hope."

Colin roared into the shaft, "Evie, I'm coming to get ye."

The only response he got was Pierre's laugh as it faded away.

Bree ran shoving Colin aside and climbed the ladder. Pierre's head appeared in the opening. A shot rang out, and Bree screamed, falling to the floor, clutching her arm.

Colin dropped and gathered Bree into his arms. "Damn it, Bree, why do ye always have to get hurt?"

Bree lifted her hand, and there was a thin line of blood. "It's only a scratch, Colin."

The pharaoh knocked Dominic aside, running toward Bree and away from the Eye of Ra. When he was almost to them, he dropped to the ground, still as death.

Everyone in the tomb stared at the mummy lying motionless on the floor.

Dominic slowly approached it and stuck the blade into the chest. A crackling sound came from the body.

Moira's eyes moved from the pharaoh to the Eye of Ra and back again. "It's the eye. The Eye of Ra powers the mummy. If he gets too far away, he has no power."

Dominic exhaled. "Well, that's a relief." He dropped the blade and dragged the dead body to the far side of the chamber, away from the Eye of Ra. "Now, how do we get out of here without getting shot?"

A voice called down from the shaft. "Miss Moira, you okay? Pierre, he's gone now. Shall I come to get you?"

Moira gasped. "Nubi. My workers." She ran to the shaft and glanced up to see Nubi's face looking down, and relief like no other washed over her. "No, Nubi, we'll head up. Get the first aid kit. We'll need it." Moira stepped back as Colin helped Bree up. What a mess, yet she felt so energized. Moira had to help these people. She had to help get Evie back.

Colin was the first to scramble up the ladder.

Bree slowly followed, only using one hand.

Colin at the top helped her out. "Come, Bree. Let's tend yer arm, love."

As she spoke, he pulled her out. "Hurry, I want to get to Evie."

Ewan moved up the ladder next. "Ma, Da, did ye see that mummy? That was so cool!" He left Moira stunned as she stood beside Dominic.

Dominic approached the ladder and stopped before Moira, who scanned the wrecked room that was once her organized dig site.

He brushed his fingers on her cheek. "Moira, are you okay?"

She sighed roughly, rubbing her arms. "Pierre took her. I can't believe he would do that."

Dominic took her into his arms and rubbed her back. Like Pierre always did, he stole one of her possessions. But this time, it was a sweet girl.

She stifled a sob. "This is all my fault, Pierre taking Evie. It's like he took something of mine, but she's your niece."

Dominic hugged her close to him and held her there for a moment.

Moira gasped and stepped back as Dominic held her in his arms. "You are really from the future. You weren't lying."

Dominic nodded as he held her.

Moira peered up the ladder and back at Dominic. "Your niece has powers. Where did those come from?"

He brushed her hair off her face. "The Fae, she's blessed by the Fae."

Moira opened her mouth to ask another question, but Dominic bent and kissed her full on the mouth.

When he stopped, Moira took a breath. "But…"

Dominic kissed her again, this time longer, making her moan. When he stopped, his eyes twinkled.

She took a deep breath, and Dominic touched her lips. "Save the questions for later, or I'll be stuck down here kissing you all day."

Moira blushed and glanced down.

Dominic started up the ladder, calling over his shoulder, "Follow me soon. I don't want you down there with that thing."

Moira started up the ladder. "His name is Psusennes I, and I don't think he wants me. He wanted Bree."

Dominic pulled Moira from the shaft to find Colin yelling at Nubi. "What do ye mean ye don't have any cars here? It's the 1930s. They have cars now."

Moira went to Nubi, who stood before an angry Colin, who was bobbing his head as he replied, "Yes, sir. And Pierre left in his car. But we only have camels. The best transportation in the desert."

Ewan tended to his mother's arm as Colin paced before Nubi.

Nubi turned to her. "Miss Moira, we do the best we can. Pierre has many men and guns again."

Moira patted his arm. "I know, Nubi. I trained you and the village workers for digs, not fighting."

Dominic snorted a laugh, and Moira shot him a look. His begging for her to hire extra help echoed in her mind. He was right. She needed protection and now even more help to retrieve Evie.

Nubi took her arm and pulled her aside. "Many things happen so fast, and many new people come. Are you well, Miss Moira?"

She sighed. "I am well. Yes, many new people appear. But we need to figure out where Pierre went, where he took young Evie."

Nubi grinned. "Mr. Pierre, he's not a bright man. He yelled to his men, so I heard. Mr. Pierre ordered his men to the airport."

Moira grabbed his arm. "Where, did he say where

they were flying to?"

Nubi nodded. "The Valley of the Kings."

Chapter 7

"We're going to the *piste,* the airstrip, the small one. We must get to the Valley of the Kings, where the enormous Eye of Ra is." Pierre spoke in his heavy French accent as the open-top car sped down the sandy desert road.

The sand burned her eyes as Evie rubbed them again. She hated this man, hated him with a passion for treating Moira so poorly. Evie hated him for taking her for what he thought were great powers. If he discovered how her Fae powers worked, she'd be in even more trouble. While she could call on her powers, she relied upon another force to gain power and had only recently started learning how to control them. She needed to think and come up with a plan. One that kept him guessing and took a long time. She wanted to give her parents time to catch up with them.

Pierre turned in his seat, directing his gaze at her. She stared out the side of the car, away from the mean man.

"Your name, girl. What is your name?"

Evie glared out the side of the car, refusing to answer him. Pierre grabbed her arm hard, making Evie cry out.

He released her arm as an idea popped into her head. "If ye keep hurting me, ye diminish my power."

Pierre grumbled, "So what am I to call you, girl?"

Evie rolled her eyes. She didn't want this man calling her anything. But she needed him to believe her. It was like playing with Doug and Ewan. She just needed to trick him like she did her brother and his friend.

She groaned, "Evie, Evie MacDougall."

Pierre nodded. "So, Evie, you can control a mummy and pull people through the Eye of Ra. What else can you do?"

Boys were dumb, and it seemed some men were as well. She didn't have that much power, but Frenchie didn't know that.

Evie smirked; this was too easy. "Depends."

Pierre squinted at her. "Depends on what? Gold, jewels. What is it, girl?"

Evie peered at him and gave him her death stare, the one that made boys shake. "Depends on what's there, what energy I can draw on. It's not always predictable. It could hurt others around me. Ones who are mean or hurt me. My hate fuels the power, and it might lash out." She curled her hand into a claw and thrashed it, making Pierre jump.

Pierre snorted. "I think you lie."

Evie grinned in her most devilish way. "Try it, old man. See what falls off yer body. A boy made me mad at school. His finger fell off." It was a lie, but the mean Frenchie didn't need to know that. He only needed to believe her.

Pierre grabbed his hands, separated them, and folded them under his legs. "I'm not *a vieillard,* an old man. Pierre is my name. You may call me that."

Evie nearly laughed out loud. But now for the convincing show. She needed a display. Evie looked around the car. She knew what she needed to show him proof of her powers. Under her foot was a rock.

She bent and picked it up. "I'll show ye one power, Mr. P." Evie showed him the rock, then handed it to him. He shied away from her as if she would hurt him.

She smiled. *Demonstrate like a magic trick, and he'll fall for it. First, gain their trust and state yer trick, the pledge. Then fold the trick, the turn. And on to the reveal, the prestige.*

He was easy bait. "Take it. Examine the rock. Make sure it's a whole rock with no cracks or breaks." The first time she'd done this with Doug, he pissed his pants. If Frenchie peed, she might not be able to hide her laugh.

Pierre reluctantly took the rock and examined it, then handed it back.

Evie took it close to her, closed her eyes, and moaned deep in her throat, trying to sound like the mummy.

Holding the rock to her chest, she peeked at Mr. P. He watched her hands with wide eyes. She grinned. Her plan worked well. Now for the dramatics.

She thrust her hands to the sky, and Mr. P jolted. "Oh, the Eye of Ra, bring me yer power, now!" She pulled the rock close and then rubbed her hands toward Mr. P, who sat back. She held the stone between her fingers and pulled the rock into two pieces. Pierre watched in stunned fascination.

"Hold out yer hands, Mr. P."

He did so, and Evie dropped the two pieces in his hands.

He held them to the sky, examining the pieces. "*Mon Dieu!*" *My God!*

The driver yelled over his shoulder, "Boss, we are almost at the airstrip."

Evie panicked. She needed to stall him. They needed to travel slower. Faking sickness worked to get out of school. She moaned and fell forward.

Pierre called out, "What is it, girl? What's the matter?"

Evie moaned louder. The fear in his voice was good. This was easier than getting out of school.

"Evie, what is it?"

She sat up slowly. "Flying. It takes away my power." She moaned, allowing her head to roll sideways as she dramatically touched her forehead. "I can't fly and keep my powers. We must travel overland."

Pierre grumbled.

The driver yelled over his shoulder, "The train leaves tonight. We can take the train, boss. We'll travel with the supplies and not have to wait until they arrive."

Pierre sighed. "*Merde! Shit!* Fine, the train." He chuckled. "After you drop us off, I need you and your partner to retrieve something for me. Something I've wanted for so long. Now that I will gain all the powers and riches of Egypt, I want Moira White."

The driver glanced over his shoulder, then back at the road. "You want us to kill her?"

Evie sucked in a breath, then covered it with a moan. Not Moira. Mr. P had it coming to him. Evie would see to it.

Pierre slapped the driver's shoulder. "No, you idiot! Bring her to me, unharmed and alive. I will finally have the young, beautiful Moira White."

He turned to Evie, who allowed her head to roll.

"This delay better be worth it, girl."

She lifted her head and held her hand out to Pierre. He raised an eyebrow, and she thrust her hand closer.

He placed both rock pieces in her hand. She laid her head back on the seat, loudly clapped her hands over her, and screamed at the top of her lungs for effect.

Pierre jumped as the driver swerved the car off the road and back into the dirt track, causing the occupants to bump into their seats.

Evie tried to hide her smile as she peered down. When she glanced up, she handed Mr. P the single rock.

He held it up, and it was whole again. *"Je serai damnée."* I'll be damned.

****

Dominic held Moira's hand as they strode behind Nubi. Nubi led them to the herd of camels that sat contently on the ground. He waved to the camels, who stared blankly as the group approached. "Here is your transportation."

Bree approached one and petted it affectionately. "Look, Colin. Camels. I love to ride."

Nubi held the bridle as Bree flung her leg over and adjusted herself. Nubi used his stick and guided the camel to stand as Bree laughed. "Oh, what fun!" It seemed Bree had ridden before. Moira's gaze followed Bree's to her husband, Colin, who folded his arms as he frowned.

Colin grunted and adjusted a handgun tucked in his belt as he approached one. "They aren't pets, Bree." He sniffed. "And they smell worse than horses."

Moira smirked. They did, but one got used to them quickly.

Nubi held the reins as Colin climbed on top. The

camel groaned and bent his head back as he tried to bite Colin's foot.

He jolted and growled. "I would have preferred cars."

Nubi moved on to Ewan, helping him as Moira climbed atop Bessie. Pulling a stick from the saddle, Moira cued her favored camel to rise. "They are sweet animals and very loyal."

Nubi stood next to Dominic before the last camel. Dominic had his rifle, revolver, and a pack of clothes with foodstuffs.

Nubi shook his head. "My camel will only carry one, Miss Moira, and certainly not all Mr. Dom has with him."

Moira used her crop, signaling Bessie to lower herself. "Dom, you can ride with me. Bessie loves carrying two. I rode her with my uncle."

Dominic strode to Moira as she eyed him. He grinned at her as he settled his rifle into the saddle. He tied his pack over the pommel but kept his revolver in his belt.

He swung his leg over the saddle and settled behind her as his arm came around her, pulling her against his chest. His light musk scent floated to her, making her stomach flutter.

His muscles shifted, and his breath blew near her ear. "It's been a while since I rode. It was just horses, but it can't be that different."

Moira turned her face to his. "It's a different gait, but you'll adjust." She turned ahead and signaled Bessie to rise.

They rocked together, and Dominic held her, bringing her body against his as he whispered in her ear, "Will you keep me comfortable, Moira?"

She giggled. "I'll see what I can do."

Nubi, now mounted, headed north. "This way. It's a few hours to the airport. I'll take the camels back when we arrive. Miss Moira, we'll keep the dig going till your return."

****

As they rode along, Dominic ran his mind through the upcoming events, approaching it like a mission. He knew he needed intel, needed to know what he faced when he came upon the mummy again. They galloped along for some time, the gait rocking them. Dominic pulled Moira closer as she handled the camel well. A woman easily taking charge without wilting under the desert heat. Dominic relaxed and mulled over his current position. He needed more information before going into anything. Pierre was a typical villain driven by greed. He'd wanted Evie's powers, so Dominic knew he'd not harm Evie. However, the living dead guy was the unknown factor in this mission to save Evie.

As the group rode at a walk, permitting the camels to rest, he spoke in Moira's ear. "So, what of our friend, the mummy? You mentioned his name, but what was he like? In life?"

He sensed her smile as she sat straighter in the saddle, her back rubbing against his front, her sweet jasmine scent tickled his nose. "Psusennes I was the third pharaoh of the twenty-first dynasty who ruled from Tanis between 1047 and 1001 BC. Psusennes is the Greek version of his original name, Pasibkhanu, which means 'The Star Appearing in the City.' " She waved her hand to the side. "In contrast, his throne name, Akheperre Setepenamun, translates as 'Great are the Manifestations of Ra, chosen of Amun.' He was the son of Pinedjem I and Henuttawy, Ramesses XI's daughter by Tentamun. He married his sister Mutnedjmet."

Bree turned to them. "You mentioned that he thought I was his sister. That's why he kissed me?"

Colin growled, "Aye, and I will take great joy in exacting revenge." Dominic smirked. Colin's protective nature always kicked in hard regarding his wife.

Ewan tilted his head back. "I wonder what kissing a mummy is like?"

Bree huffed a laugh. "It was like licking musty sand—dry and tasted bad."

Ewan scrunched his face. "Ewww."

Dominic grinned to himself. Bree's kids were entertaining. But he still needed more information. "What about the man? What was he like?"

Moira sighed. "I can only tell you what history wrote of his time. During his long reign, Psusennes built the enclosure walls and the central part of the Great Temple at Tanis, which he dedicated to the Amun, Mut, and Khonsu triad. Psusennes was the ruler responsible for turning Tanis into a capital city, surrounding its temple with a formidable brick *temenos* wall. He built a sanctuary dedicated to Amun composed of blocks salvaged from the derelict Pi-Ramesses. Many of these blocks were unaltered and kept the name of Pi-Ramesses' builder, Ramesses II, including obelisks still bearing the name of Ramesses II transported from the former capital of Pi-Ramesses to Tanis."

Dominic blew out his breath. "Nothing of the man letting us know if he's good or evil?"

Colin rode close, eyeing him, and nodded. Dominic was right to ask. Did the dead pharaoh have evil inside of him that an evil Fae could use to their advantage? Was this part of going after a Stone of Iona, or was this only the mummy's curse?

Colin leaned over. "We talk later."

Dominic nodded, hoping Colin had some insight that would help.

The distinctive pattern of a horse galloping came to him from a distance.

Dominic turned, and two men approached fast on horses from the east.

Moira pulled up till her camel stopped, and the rest of the group followed. Shots rang out, and the camels jolted.

Dominic cursed himself. He'd allowed his defenses down and had not taken note of his surroundings, figuring, "What could happen in the middle of the desert?" This wasn't the twenty-first century. There wouldn't be a war here for a long time. But here he sat, being fired at while on a camel in the middle of the desert.

Nubi rode past them. "It's Pierre's men, miss."

Dominic grabbed the reins and spun the camel to survey the area—no one else was in sight. Shots rang out again as the horses came closer.

Colin rode to him. "The mountain to our right. We are closer than the men on horseback."

Dominic turned, spying the rocky ridge. "Good call, Colin."

Colin turned in his saddle as another shot came at them. "Bree, Ewan! Ye ride on ahead." He spun his camel as Nubi, Bree, and Ewan rode past and toward the hillside.

Dominic rode beside Colin as they followed the group up the hillside. He pulled his revolver out but struggled to hold the reins and the gun.

Moira grabbed the reins. "You shoot. I'll drive."

The camels galloped along on their bumpy gate, making it hard for Dominic to aim. The horses quickly caught up as one man in a white shirt approached them. He reached up and grabbed at Moira, who screamed. She shied away, nearly falling off the camel.

Dominic grabbed her closer to him and righted them on the saddle. "Moira, I have you!"

The other attacker in all black came up to the left and tried to grab Moira. He grabbed her leg as she screamed. Another shot rang out, and the man in black on the left fell from his horse, letting go of Moira. The man in the white shirt slowed and fell behind.

Not looking back, Dominic steered them to the hillside, rode up it, and didn't stop till they were with Nubi and the others.

He swung from the saddle with Moira in his arms. "Are you hurt? Did a bullet hit you?" He ran his hands along her body, checking for any wounds, and found none. She hugged him close, shaking as her wide eyes met his. Dominic guessed this was the first time Pierre or his men had shot at her.

Colin rode into the clearing and stopped his camel. "Is everyone okay?"

Nubi waved his stick, and Colin's camel sat as Colin slid from the saddle.

He strode to Bree, who ran into his arms. "Colin, are you all right? I heard shots."

He nodded. "Aye, we are fine." His gaze connected

with Dominic's. "They were after Moira. I shot one in the leg. That's what made them pull back."

Ewan ran to his parents. "Da, ye shot one?"

Colin nodded, his eyes still on Dominic, who shifted Moira in his arms. "Moira, they were after you. Why?" His eyes swung to hers.

She shrugged and looked down. "It's nothing, Dom."

Nubi huffed. "Pierre always wanted her. We protect her, but the Frenchman desires her."

Moira pushed against Dominic, but he held her tighter. "No, I'm staying by your side. I told you. *You* needed more help and better protection. Now you will have it." Damn, the Frenchman disgusted him.

Bree sniffled. "He won't hurt Evie, will he?"

Colin brushed her hair away from her face. "No, Bree, he needs her. But standing here won't rescue her."

Nubi called from the cliffside. "They gone now, Miss Moira. Back to Cairo. It's safe now."

Dominic rose, holding Moira in his arms. "Come on, dear. Time to ride."

Moira whispered in Dominic's ear, "I hope we get to her in time."

Chapter 8

After another hour in the saddle, they arrived at the small airport. Colin pulled Dominic aside as Moira approached the government officials at the airport in Tanis, Egypt. Knowing her ability to find trouble inadvertently, Dominic stepped aside while he kept Moira in sight. Speaking to a government official, she'd likely get arrested for asking to travel. He needed to keep an eye on her.

Colin spoke lowly. "Now that we can speak away from Moira, I need to update ye on the Fae fable."

Dominic glanced at Colin. "The book turned, and a fable showed? Wait, you guys were in Florida?"

His eye trailed back to Moira as Colin replied, "Aye, both Fae sisters came to us with the book. They explained the shortened version of a long fable. If ye would call it a shortened version. Damn things get longer with each one they reveal."

Dominic spied Moira's huff when her loose hair flew up as the government official spoke. "Okay, go on, Colin."

Colin rubbed his neck, then looked up. "Something about two brothers arguing over land, their dad dying as the oldest brother's son searched the world for the Stone of Hope. He ended up in Egypt with an old hag and fed her. She turned into his true love, and he found the stone."

Bree spoke from behind Colin. "That's the story but not the quote, Colin."

Colin pinched his nose without turning. "Why can't ye ever stay where I tell ye? Ye were supposed to stay with Ewan."

Dominic kept his eyes on Moira, who folded her arms as she spoke to the official.

Ewan stepped beside him. "Ma didn't leave me, and she's right. There are two quotes from that fable ye must remember. They are, 'The hope of the righteous is gladness; the expectation of the wicked perishes,' and 'But those who have hope will renew their strength. They will run and not grow weary; they will walk and not be faint; they will soar like wings on eagles.' "

Without taking his eyes off a frustrated Moira, Dominic spoke. "Ewan, you and Evie discussed the fable the first night here and mentioned the quotes matched Moira's Egypt story."

Bree shifted under her husband's arm until he wrapped it around her. "Yes, I said the same when I heard Moira speak it in the burial chamber."

Ewan nodded. "Aye, Evie said she saw the Stone of Hope in the portal and that we were meant to be here." He sighed. "Evie said that's what made her lose concentration and control of the portal." He turned to his father, Colin. "She's sorry, Da."

He rubbed Ewan's head. "That's okay, son. We all lose focus at times. But when did ye memorize the fable's quotes? The book's in the case."

Ewan glanced down. "Brigid made Evie and me memorize nearly all the fables. Brigid can make the case disappear. At first, it was fun, but later it was a chore."

Colin snorted. "I'll wring that damn sprite's neck for all she's done to ye kids."

Ewan's head shot up. "Don't be mad, Da. Brigid said our generation needed a fighting chance. I am glad to have the information that we need now."

Dominic kept his eye on Moira now that she waved her arms and spoke louder to the official. "Ewan, you have heard both stories of the Divine Family and the Stone of Hope. Tell us, what are the connections between them?"

"Moira's story is about Horus' parents and how he argued with his uncle over the land in Egypt. The quote, 'But those who have hope will renew their strength. They will run and not grow weary; they will walk and not faint; they will soar like wings on eagles.' It is in it, but not the other Brigid told Evie and me to memorize." He took a breath. "The second is 'The hope of the righteous is gladness; the expectation of the wicked perishes.' "

Bree tilted her head. "The second is the curse to the mummy. Moira mentioned it in the chamber."

Dominic spoke as Moira shook her head at the official. "So, it's the relatives arguing over land that are the same. You said Evie saw the stone. What's it look like?"

Ewan nodded. "Green in a rectangle, like a long rectangle." His head shot up. "The stone, it's broken in two like the Fae fable."

Dominic's gaze went to Ewan. "Evie's trick with the stone. She can break them and put them back whole again."

Colin growled, "And now we know why we are all here. Damn Brigid and her games."

Dominic turned as Moira strode to them with a heated look in her eye. "Moira approaches. I've only told her we are from the future but nothing about the stones and the Fae."

Ewan smirked. "Was that before or after ye threw her to the ground and kissed her?" Dominic almost laughed aloud. The twins spied on him and Moira. He should have known as much, sneaky little rugrats!

Bree gasped, and Colin chuckled as Moira stepped into the group.

****

Moira huffed and folded her arms across her chest. "That damn man, he's at it again. Bribing the officials to keep me out of everything. They won't allow me to fly."

Dominic pulled her closer to him as he spoke to Colin. "Ah, cut you off all travel." He peeked around, and Moira followed his gaze. More government men were at the small airfield than usual. She blew a sigh. Dominic rubbed her back, and she relaxed.

Colin chuckled near her, his eyes on Dominic's hand at her back.

She glanced back as Dominic spoke. "Even more difficult is that we have no papers, passports, or identification. This is going to be harder than I thought."

Ewan shifted closer to the group and spoke lowly. "Uncle Dom, if I can change the man's mind. Get us on the tarmac. Can ye pilot a plane?"

Colin frowned at Ewan as Dominic nodded. "I can fly anything. Wait, what do you mean, change his mind?"

Ewan shrugged and scuffed his toe. "Ye know,

change his mind…for him."

Dominic studied the tarmac and then turned back to Ewan. "You can do that?"

Ewan beamed at his uncle. "Aye, it's easy as long as the person is weak-minded."

Colin folded his arms, glaring at his son. "And exactly how did ye find out ye had these powers, Ewan?"

The brother has powers, too. What is it with this family? Moira frowned.

Ewan glanced away and back at his father. "Well, one day, I just thought a thought I wanted. The person that I wanted to do something, well, they did what my mind told them when they didn't want to."

His father glared at him. "Explain and leave no detail out."

Ewan squinted at his mother, then his father. "The big assignment in English I didn't do last year. Well, I made the teacher believe I did it. Got an A."

Ewan grinned as Moira laughed, then covered her mouth as the others glared at her. What she wouldn't give to have powers like that. Pierre wouldn't be an issue at all. No one would be an issue.

Colin growled and turned to Bree, who studied the ceiling.

He gasped. "Ye knew, didn't ye?"

She peeked at her husband. "Of course, I knew. Who do you think helped him learn to control it?"

Colin pointed his finger at Ewan.

Dominic grabbed it, lowering his arm. "Just this once. He'll use it to get us on the tarmac, but I didn't see a plane large enough for all five of us." He turned to Ewan. "Do you need an interpreter? You don't speak

Arabic."

Ewan smiled. "I'll be one with his mind. It comes out in my head as my language. Convenient, isn't it?"

Colin glared at his son. "Ye have not used this power on yer parents, have ye, Ewan? On me?"

Bree snickered as Ewan rolled his eyes. "It doesn't work. Ye and Ma are strong-minded. Believe me, I tried."

Moira covered her smile with her hand. This family banter was something she sorely missed. Being around Dominic's family reminded her of all she missed and longed for in a family.

Colin turned to Dominic. "Okay, if ye can't find one large enough for all of us, ye two get on the plane, and we'll—improvise."

Ewan beamed, folding his arms. "I can probably get us on the train. I've done it for my friends before."

Colin glared at Ewan. "I shudder to think the trouble ye have gotten into with this power."

Ewan strolled to the government official and spoke lowly to him as he waved his hand in front of the man's face. How Ewan spoke Arabic amazed Dominic, but this mind control power was new.

The government official blinked at Ewan and then at the group behind him. "You can go to the tarmac."

Ewan glanced back, grinning as Colin leaned down, whispering to Bree, "We'll be discussing this later."

Bree smirked and patted his cheek. "Yes, dear."

Moira exchanged a look with Dominic, who shrugged. She suspected Colin would forget and figured Bree planned never to bring it up again. She liked this family more and more.

They made their way to the closest plane. Dominic eyed the area, and Moira followed his gaze. "They both look the same."

Dominic sighed. "They are. Old army planes, two-seaters. Easy enough."

He turned to a frowning Colin. "I take it, Colin, you can't fly a plane."

Colin huffed a laugh. "Not unless I grow wings. Ye take Moira and fly. Bree, Ewan, and I will catch up on a train. This way, Moira can lead ye to where that dammed Frenchman took Evie." He took Bree's hand and nudged his son ahead of him. "If ye can get close— grab her. But not if he's going to hurt her."

Bree gasped as Colin pulled her away. "Colin, Evie won't get hurt, will she?" Their voices faded the farther away Colin took them. "No, lass…"

Dominic turned to Moira. "Up on the plane with you." Dominic lifted Moira to the step on the side of the aircraft. She'd never sat at the controls before and had flown only twice.

Moira gasped. "You're going to fly this?"

Dominic grinned at her. "Easy as pie and just as sweet."

A man called out to them in Arabic, "Hey, you, get off of the craft."

Moira gasped. "He said—"

Dominic pushed her up the steps. "I know what he said. I have this whole time."

She climbed up the steps.

Dominic glanced over his shoulder. "Crap, get in and punch the red button to start the plane." He ran off, calling over his shoulder, "I'll move the wheelbases. *Don't* touch anything else."

Moira nodded as she climbed onto the plane. When she sat down and studied the instrument console, her mind went blank. There were so many dials, levers, and gauges. Red, she remembered red. She pushed a red button, and the plane's engine started.

She turned, and Dominic moved beside the wheel. As her knee hit a lever, the aircraft turned to the right. She cried out, and the man chasing Dominic ducked under the wing as it passed over him.

Dominic yelled, "Damn it, Moira! What have you done?"

She turned to her left, and Dominic tried to climb up the side of the plane to the seat in front of her. "I don't know, Dom!"

As the plane rotated, the man chasing Dominic pulled on his leg. Dominic kicked him, and he fell to the ground. The plane's wheel ran over him, forcing the plane to lurch.

The movement jolted Moira in her seat, and she hit the lever again. The plane jumped forward, jostling Dominic. His left arm and foot flung out as he held on to the side of the aircraft with one hand.

Gunshots rang out, and Moira yelped.

As Dominic climbed onto the plane, he yelled over the engine, "Don't touch anything else, Moira. You're going to get us killed."

She yelled back, "I'm sorry. I've never been a pilot."

More gunshots sounded. Moira cried out and ducked.

Dominic got into the seat before her and yelled over his shoulder, "Well, thank God I am. Buckle up, honey. It might be a bumpy takeoff."

Moira found the seat belt and fastened herself in. "Are you sure you know how to fly this?"

Dominic laughed. "Honey, I can fly anything." He steered them around as more gunfire ran out, and he lined the plane with the runway. He slowed the plane down and revved the engine.

Moira's panic rose. "Why are we stopping? They're still shooting at us."

Dominic yelled over the roar of the engine, "Not enough runway. I need more power, or we won't make liftoff." He leaned forward as the engine roared. The plane jolted forward and picked up speed.

Dominic laughed as he yelled out, "Come on, baby. You can make it. Give me more."

Moira leaned sideways and gaped out the front.

The buildings at the end of the runway drew closer. "Dom, Dom. We need to go up."

Dominic yelled back, "I know, honey. I'm working on it."

The buildings came closer, and the plane wasn't lifting.

Moira screamed. "Dominic!" As the plane's nose tilted up, she sensed the lift. When they climbed into the sky, the gunfire faded.

Dominic turned the plane right, heading south. Moira gazed out over the side. The view of Tanis' ruins under the plane cast shadows of the last remnants of a once thriving city. She spotted her campsite and dig area and prayed Pierre was well away. Nubi and the villagers would continue the excavation work while she took a brief detour to rescue Evie.

Her eyes traveled to her left and the city of Cairo, Egypt, glimmering in the distance. Now, it was a thriving metropolis and capital of Egypt. The Sphinx and pyramids set a frame of the past against the city of the new, making Moira wonder what the future might hold.

She turned, looking at Dominic, confident and carefree as he easily flew the aircraft. He turned his head toward the afternoon sun, lighting his tanned face while the wind ruffled his wavy hair. Charismatic and a warrior at heart. She could easily envision future women falling at his feet. Yet he was in Egypt in the 1930s with his niece and nephew. He was well-loved by his sister and her family. What would a man from the future see in the homely scholar from the past?

Moira sighed.

Dominic turned to her and smiled as he nodded to the view. "See, easy as pie and just as sweet."

****

Later that night, on the train, Pierre's thugs left Evie in the cabin with a guard at the door. Pierre went to the club car to drink. She was content to be alone. They'd converted the area from seating for four to sleeping beds. She had slipped off her shoes and slept in her clothing, not having anything else available. As long as she kept Mr. P believing if he hurt her, her powers diminished, she hoped he'd leave her alone. She gazed out the window, watching the darkness of the night descend upon the land. The purple hues against the orange setting sun spread out across the darkening landscape made her heart ache for home. But most of all, she missed her parents.

She must have dozed off for a bit, and she jolted awake to find the boy in all-white sitting across from her. She sat up suddenly, glancing at the door. The guard still stood leaning against it.

She spoke as she turned to him. "How did ye…"

The boy winked. "Tricks, like ye play on Mr. P, Evie."

She huffed. "Ye helped me earlier with the portal."

The boy switched seats, sitting next to her. "Aye, I did."

Evie shifted, allowing him space to sit. "Ye are a Fae, like Brigid. What's yer name?"

He grinned. "I cannot speak my name aloud in this realm, but ye may call me friend."

Evie nodded and beheld the scenery.

The boy shifted closer to her, taking her hand in his. "Ye seem lonely and sad. May I tell ye a story to pass the time? It will make ye happy."

Evie turned to the boy, then glanced at his hand, holding hers. It was warm and felt good.

She nodded and leaned back, watching the landscape fly by as the train sped along.

The boy leaned back next to her and gazed out the window as he whispered in her ear, "There once was a Fae. A Fae prince born as grandson to the great king of the good Fae, the Tuatha Dé Danann. His mother and father rejoiced at the birth of their son with exceptional gifts that few Fae have."

Evie exhaled. "What gifts?"

The boy's grin came through in the tone of his response. "Some powerful, some sweet, some scary. The power he held was vast. He trained in his youth to control these powers since they could cause great harm if misused."

Evie looked at him, and he smiled. "The Fae boy, he had many dreams. Some made sense, and some did not. One dream, in particular, was of a girl. A human girl."

Evie blushed and gazed at their hands. He caressed hers as he held it. "When he woke, he couldn't remember what the girl looked like, only how she made him feel."

Evie peeked at his face. "How did she make him feel?"

The boy sighed. "Tingly, warm, happy. Whole." The boy frowned and glanced at their hands. "He knew how she made him feel but could never see her face. His mother, a powerful Fae, searched the land far and wide to find his dream girl. She never found her. His father searched as well, to no avail."

Evie stared as the boy peeked up at her. "It wasn't until he had a vision of her through the Eye of Ra that he saw her face for the first time. Then he knew who she was." He leaned in, their faces close.

Evie whispered, "Who was she?"

The boy replied, "The girl of his dreams."

He kissed her lightly on the lips. Holding her hand in his, he slid his other hand around her and pulled her closer, holding her in his embrace. He kissed her again, this time deeper.

A boy had kissed Evie once, but it was wet and flat. This soft, warm kiss moved her as they breathed together. Butterflies fluttered in her chest, and her stomach did a flip.

Evie gasped, and the boy slid his tongue into her mouth. She was light and hot at once as she eagerly returned his kisses.

He slowly ended the kiss and held Evie as they lounged together, watching the land at night speed by.

After some time, the boy sat up, staring at the door, then turned to Evie. "I must go. Someone comes."

Evie let out a whimper. She didn't want him to go.

He peered at her, and she sensed he didn't want to leave.

With a twist of his wrist, a ball of light formed. He shifted, handing it to her.

She watched the light, mesmerized.

He spoke, breaking the spell. "Take the light, Evie."

She held her hand out, and he carefully placed the small ball of light into her hand. It warmed like when he held her hand. She sighed in wonder.

"Close yer hand around it and place it by yer heart."

Evie did so, and it warmed her body as the light faded.

"When ye want to call me to ye, think of me. Twist yer wrist as I did, and the light will glow. I will come at yer call."

She closed her eyes and held on to the ball. It slowly vanished, as did the boy. Evie curled up, content and safe. Even Mr. P arriving and stumbling around the cabin next door didn't deter her mood. She pretended to sleep, and eventually, Mr. P's loud snores filled the space. She dreamt of the boy, the boy of her dreams.

Chapter 9

Near sunset, Dominic landed their plane beside Nubi's home village, New Gourna. Moira had suggested the location to keep them away from the airport, as Pierre had likely bribed government agents to stop Moira from traveling. It seemed he'd blocked her before, and she didn't doubt he'd block her again. At first, Dominic rejected her idea, skeptical that he could land on the firm sand. But the long stretch of open land proved a perfect landing spot.

Dominic went to the plane as the village leader, Mamduh, welcomed them warmly, hugging Moira. "Miss come back. We are happy to have you."

She hugged him back. "Mamduh, Pierre brings trouble again. Has he shown himself near the Valley of the Kings?"

Mamduh shook his head. "I didn't know we must look for him. I'll let our people know to look out for the Frenchman."

His eyes roamed to Dominic as he set rocks against the plane's wheels, securing the aircraft. "And a new friend." Mamduh shook Dominic's hand when he approached. "A warrior you bring. Nambi has food ready. Come, come. We visit." He was a warrior, yet natural and at ease in the simple village.

Nubi's wife, Nambi, waved to them before her small hut. A pot was already over the cookfire outside,

100

as usual. When Nambi lifted the lid, the scent of familiar spiced meat reached Moira, making her stomach growl.

Spooning portions into bowls, Nambi handed them to each person as they sat on rocks outside the one-room home Moira often visited in Nubi's village. Next, Nambi made the rounds with spiced hot tea. Moira dug in, starved from the week's activities.

As Moira watched the sunset, Dominic picked at his dish. "What is this? It smells good but looks—" He held up a serving on a fork. "—suspicious." He smelled it again. "In Saudi, I had *mutabbaq*, a spicy folded omelet stuffed with ground vegetables and meat. But not this."

Moira spoke after swallowing some spiced tea. "*Koshari*. An unusual combination of mixed lentils, macaroni noodles, and rice in a single dish that they top with a spicy tomato sauce that uses a special Middle Eastern spice blend." She held up her fork. "Oh, and garbanzo beans and fried onions. The idea sounds strange…until you taste it." She took another bite, humming. "Try it. Then you'll know why Egyptians and tourists fondly speak of 'The Koshari Man,' the title bestowed upon street vendors who sell the dish from their carts. But Nambi's is better."

Nambi blushed as she ate with the group.

Dominic ate a bite, then another. He seemed to enjoy the dish, or his hunger won over.

Dominic spoke between bites. "Mamduh, your village is very nice. Thank you for allowing us to stay." Moira grinned, glad Dominic had given the proper cultural welcome, thanks, and compliments. How much travel had this man from the future done?

Mamduh smiled. "Anything for Miss Moira. She brings us work." He bowed his head to her. "All that we have is because of her."

Moira blushed as Mamduh's gaze settled on Dominic. "Before Moira and her uncle Ben, Pierre brought most of the business to villagers who wanted to work the digs for Egypt's treasures." He shook his head. "Pierre hires at such low wages. We can't support ourselves." He snorted. "Pierre's treatment of his workers is what Miss calls slave labor."

Dominic studied Moira as she turned away with a firm set on her mouth. So, she and her uncle hated Pierre's methods. With good reason.

Mamduh's voice came softer. "But when Uncle Ben partnered with Pierre and asserted the change in wage and treatment, Pierre changed his ways. Others followed suit, making the conditions better. Then, when Uncle Ben insisted the treasures go to museums, everyone in Egypt wanted to become a part. A part of sharing Egypt's treasures with the world." He sighed. "It seemed the Gods smiled upon them as things were good for a while." His expression grew grim. "But Pierre, he's not an honorable man. He stole and sold items to collectors. Some say he made the Gods angry." Mamduh fisted his hand. "Uncle Ben and Pierre argued a lot. Then Ben died." He bowed his head as Moira sniffled. "But Moira, she gives us hope. She gives all of Egypt hope by bringing back and sharing the treasures that please the Gods."

Mamduh folded his hands together in prayer. Moira prayed her work did please the Gods.

Moira looked away. "It wasn't all that much."

Dominic snorted. "I doubt that very much. Your

battle against Pierre seems to have brewed long before today. Hell, long before your uncle died." He studied Mamduh. "Moira is such a strong woman and, with help, could accomplish so much more."

Mamduh opened his eyes and nodded.

Moira rose. "Come, Dominic. I'll show you my hut they keep for me." She stood, and Dominic followed.

She stopped them and bowed to Nambi, who had taken their plates. "Thank you for the meal, Nambi. It was quite delicious." He followed her lead and then nodded to Mamduh.

Both holding their tea, Moira led him past several huts to one off to the side.

A villager stood before the house, and when they approached, he nodded to Moira. "All's ready, Miss. Have a nice night."

Moira nodded to the villager, then turned and waved to Dominic. "Let's sit before the fire."

He situated himself against a rock before the warm fire and sat back, sipping tea and staring at the final rays of the sun. She sat next to him, content to enjoy the end of the day in good company.

Dominic's eyes wandered through the village and then landed on the hut. "The huts aren't much different from adobe homes in New Mexico. Mud bricks made from local dirt and covered with a smooth mud mixture forming a smooth surface on the outside, something which could withstand the elements of the climate." He turned to her. "Very efficient use of natural resources, and they stay cool in the day and warm at night."

They sat side by side, close, and she shivered, then rubbed her arms for warmth as they sat in silent companionship. Dominic shifted and embraced her, cradling her with his body's heat. His chest shook as he chuckled, and his musk scent came to her, comforting her.

She glanced at him as he smirked at the flames of the fire. "What, what is so funny?"

He peered at her and smirked. "No gin to keep you warm tonight."

She chuckled. "If I had any tonight, I might not share."

Dominic chuckled. "Well, I'd share my portion with you."

She shivered again. "I don't understand why I never grew accustomed to the chill. It never bothered my uncle." She settled closer into his embrace as he squeezed her once, making her feel cherished.

His chest vibrated as he spoke. "Tell me of him, your uncle."

Moira sighed. She loved her uncle and missed him deeply. "He was a great archeologist, probably the best." She blew a short laugh. "He was a better Egyptologist than most Egyptians. Most deferred to his knowledge without question."

Dominic rubbed his hand slowly up and down her arm as she spoke, and she warmed against him. "How did he get tangled up with the Frenchman, Pierre?"

Anger raced through her, thinking of Pierre, all he took from her, her finds, her accomplishments—the last of her family, her uncle. Pierre was the one thing she could not conquer, like a sickness that never cured, no matter how hard she tried.

Moira took a deep breath. "That's a simple answer: money. Pierre had the money to fund the digs, and my uncle had the brains to find them. It was through my uncle that Pierre cultivated his relationship with the Egyptian government. Which he now uses against me." She snorted. "It's as if I suddenly don't exist for the Egyptian government. Before his death, they recognized my efforts alongside my uncle for years." She fisted her hand and hit it against her leg. "It's so frustrating. Pierre has them thinking he's placing the antiquities he finds in European museums. But really, he sells them to the highest bidders for private collections. He hires local labor at lower than trade rates and treats his workers more like slaves rather than people."

Dominic spoke low, an edge to his voice. "Why don't you complain? Tell the government what he's really doing?"

She shifted and scowled at him. "I have! They treat me like they don't see me because I am a woman."

Dominic caressed her face. "Well, I see you. I see you for the intelligence you have. For the hard work you do." The wind blew a wayward auburn, wiry curl across her face, and before she could reach for it, Dominic eased it behind her ear. "I see you as the strong, courageous woman you are." He bent his head toward hers and kissed her lightly on the lips. He studied her face as if trying to memorize the shape, capturing her image to hold.

She peered over his face, the angled jawline with a day's growth of stubble making him seem more like a warrior than the military man he was. To her, he was her warrior, her protector against all the evils in the world. What would it be like to open her heart to a man like Dominic, to give herself to him?

He kissed her again, and she sighed into his mouth.

He tilted his mouth over hers and deepened the kiss as their tongues danced. Moira gave in and became lost. She didn't think, only felt.

As Dominic slid his hand over her breast, Moira moaned. He cupped the roundness of it as he continued to kiss her deeply. Butterflies fluttered in her stomach, and her breath hitched. No man had touched her this way, and she now understood what women meant when they talked about not being able to resist a man. As he continued the assault on her senses, Moira gripped his shoulders as if her life depended on it.

Dominic grinned into this kiss and flipped them over so she lay beneath him with the soft sand against her back. He slid his leg between hers, rubbing his leg against her as he kissed her again. As Dominic undid the buttons of her shirt, the cool night air moved across her chest. Before she could catch her next breath, his hand pulled her breast from her bra and pinched the nipple to a firm peak. Moira moaned as she arched into his caress, and he slid the other breast free. Dominic flicked his tongue over the nipple as Moira nearly came undone.

She ran her hands over his chest, wanting desperately to have it bare as hers was.

As if reading her mind, Dominic rose slightly and smiled as he pulled his button-down shirt over his head. She grinned, sat up a little, and repeated the same with her shirt. When she sat up, Dominic reached behind her, unclasped her bra, and tossed it aside. Moira leaned forward, her bare chest rubbing against his, the friction of his chest hairs sending tingles from her chest to her toes. Dominic chuckled and reached up to unpin her hair as she leaned over and kissed him fully. She gazed into his face as he pulled her hair down, running his hands through it. His eyes followed her long auburn curls as they fell around her in long, flowing waves.

He flipped the long length over her shoulder, covering one breast. "God, I have wanted to see your hair undone ever since I first saw you."

Moira blushed and glanced down. "When you first saw me, I was covered in dirt in the tomb."

Dominic still played with her hair, the firelight flickering over the red highlights.

He gazed into her eyes. "No, the first time I saw you was through the eye before we came through. You turned, and I saw you for the first time." He brushed a kiss against her lips as he curled her hair around his hand. "You seemed so vulnerable. I just wanted to reach out and touch you like I am now."

He rotated their bodies and lay on his back as she sat on his hips. He spread her hair around her shoulders, allowing it to fall over her chest, then parting it and placing his hands on her breasts. His shaft pulsed against her, a new sensation for her. She rocked forward a little and jolted at the feeling. Dominic rocked in response, making Moira throw her head back and moan. No man had ever touched her like this, and she didn't want any other man to touch her this way ever.

Dominic sat up, gathering her in his arms. "God, Moira, what you do to me." He shifted her in his lap and, as he rose to his knees, lifted her, cradling her in his arms as he stood. He strode into their hut, needing to duck as he went inside. He stood still momentarily as their eyes adjusted to the dim light from the single lantern beside the bed. Dominic turned as the light shone from behind him, casting his face in shadow and hers in light. He slowly lowered her down his body as his muscular body molded against hers. He held her in his arms, gazing into her eyes.

She didn't move, and she couldn't if she wanted to. Dominic smiled and peered down, then back at her face. "Moira, I do not wish to frighten you." He brushed a curl from her face and softly kissed her lips.

She responded quickly, deepening the embrace. She could not get enough of Dominic's kisses—enough of him.

Between kisses, Dominic whispered, "Moira, I want…" He kissed her. "God, Moira…"

She kissed him again as he spoke into the kiss. "Moira, I want you…"

He kissed her deeply. "May I make love to you?"

Moira sighed. "I would love that, Dom, please?"

He trailed kisses down her neck till he sucked a nipple into his mouth. His hands fumbled, then freed her pants. He lowered them as he knelt at her feet making quick work of untying her boot laces. He pulled her boots off one by one as she stepped out of them. He rose before her as her hair freely flowed around her, partially covering her chest.

Dominic regarded her body, now bare before him, lit in the low light from the lantern. "Beautiful. You are so beautiful."

He moved forward, swept her into his arms again, and stepped to the bed as he gently lowered her to the mattress. He shifted back and stripped down his pants and kicked his boots off. His honed body took Moira's breath with its sheer masculine beauty. Muscles rippled as he climbed onto the bed and lay beside her, taking her into his arms again. She rubbed her hand down his chest, reveling in the springy texture of his hair.

Dominic kissed her deeply, and it seemed he poured all his feelings into that one kiss. His hand slid up her leg and covered her as her hips involuntarily rose to meet his caress. He kissed her and rubbed his finger along her till it was moist, making her moan.

She was wet, and she floated as he caressed her more. She gripped his shoulders tighter as he slid a finger inside as her walls gripped him. He moved his mouth to her nipple as he worked his finger. She had the sensation inside her of climbing, but for what? She wasn't sure. His finger quickened the pace as he returned to kissing her mouth, and her hips bucked as the world around her exploded in one quick burst of energy. Dominic's finger kept up the rapid pace as she cried out, and flashes of light flashed behind her eyelids. She floated as if she flew to the stars. So high she couldn't catch her breath. As her breathing returned to normal, Dominic shifted beside her. He lightly kissed her cheek, then her lips.

She blinked and grinned as he chuckled. "Liked that, did you?"

She turned to him. "That was wondrous, but I know that's not all."

Dominic caressed her cheek. "No, sweet Moira. That's just the beginning. I wanted to ensure you were ready. I suspected this would be your first time."

She blushed and tried to look down, but Dominic caught her chin. "I want to make love to you, and I want you to enjoy it. It will initially hurt, but please trust me; it will improve."

She smiled, and he kissed her as he shifted over

and between her legs. He kissed her deeper as he slid into her juices, wetting them both. The familiar sensation rose within her again, and he continued to rock, rubbing himself against her. He caressed one breast and then the other while kissing her and swaying in a rhythm that built the energy inside her again. He increased the pace and pressure, and she moaned as her hips bucked.

Dominic rose above her, watching her face, and with the next shift, he slowly slid inside. He stopped halfway. He caressed her face and kissed her as he gazed into her eyes. She saw the tension in him and reached up to touch his face. He slowly slid farther and broke her barrier in a quick thrust. She sucked in a breath at the sharp pain, but Dominic kissed her as she let it out, and he slid in to the hilt. She sighed as his fullness made her feel complete. Dominic shifted and slid out as she gasped at the friction, and he slid in again.

The intense, full feeling brought out a moan. Dominic kissed her deeply as he picked up his rhythm, and that energy built again inside her. They moaned together as Dominic increased the pace. The fullness hit her at just the right point, making her hips buck again. These wild sensations overwhelmed her, the feelings all over her body, the tingling, the hot and cold all at once. It was too much for Moira.

Dominic kept the pace and kissed her again as the energy built, and she couldn't take it anymore.

She screamed his name into the night as he drove a thrust deep into her, held it there as her walls pulsed around him. He pushed into her again, and the last time, he rose on his arms, arching into the night, calling her name. When he gathered her into his arms, their bodies were still connected. He panted heavily, as did she. She still floated in the stars as he kissed her neck, whispering her name repeatedly.

On a moan, Dominic slowly separated their bodies. The movement jolted her awake. She must have dozed. He whispered "shhh" and curved her into his arms.

He pulled a cover over them and spoke low in her ear. "Moira, sweet Moira. I never want to let you go."

Chapter 10

Dominic turned, spying Moira across the market aisle in Luxor, Egypt, examining a fruit vendor's goods. That morning, the villagers gave them clothing to blend in with the people of Luxor. Moira wore a dress called an abaya, a headscarf called the hijab, which included a face cover, much like the village women. White, yet it accentuated her tanned skin. She was beautiful.

Dominic wore a white tunic with pants, but much longer for his height, with a turban around his head. He never imagined wearing this clothing in all his days, but he did for Moira.

The vendor tapped his arm, speaking in Arabic. "Sir, you like the knife. A fair price of three hundred pounds." Still outraged at the currency exchange rate, Dominic paid for the large knife with a fist full of Egyptian pounds Moira gave him. He eyed the bill, surprised that it held a watermark in the 1930s. The image of the Sphinx took up most of the design. The watermark impressed him as he flipped the bill over. The other side bore the picture of the King Tutankhamun as a youth.

He paid the merchant and shoved the knife in his belt beside his revolver. He smirked; the more time he spent in Moira's company, the more weapons he accumulated. She seemed to need protection.

He moved beside her as she went to the jeweler

and eyed earrings. "Want a pair?" She set them down and stepped away, whispering, "They are tin and a bad copy of a set I found last year."

He hummed as they walked side by side, strolling through the market. "If you don't mind me asking, what happened to your parents?"

She sighed. "I don't mind, and it was years ago." She glanced at him. "I was ten. They were in a car accident on the way home from a party."

An image of a 1934 burgundy coupe he'd seen at an auto show flashed in his mind: the big headlights, the convertible top, thin glass, and bucket seats. No seat belts. He shuddered at the idea of what a high-speed accident might do to people inside.

She lifted her face to the wind. "Uncle Ben was my mom's brother. When he came to the funeral, I left with him." She shrugged. "Been here ever since."

He took her hand in his as they strolled. "I am sorry for your loss." She leaned her head on his arm as he held her hand. "You know, I lost my parents as well."

Moira turned to him. "Really?"

He nodded as he squeezed her hand. "Not together. My father died when we were young. Brielle likely remembers better than I, being older. I have a hard time remembering him without pictures." He exhaled. "But my mom, well, that was more recent."

Moira stopped him and took both his hands in hers. "Tell me."

The crowd faded, and Dominic stared into her hazel-green eyes. He'd not discussed it with anyone—didn't want to. But here with her, he had the urge to unburden himself, wanting to share this with someone compassionate and who would understand.

"The short times I'd spent with my mom were hard. Her battle with cancer was brutal and took its toll on her."

Moira tilted her head. "Cancer? Do you mean those tumors they can't get rid of? I've heard those are terrible."

Dominic nodded. He didn't think she'd know what cancer was, but it seemed she did. "When the chance came to join the military, fighting, I jumped at it, burying myself there instead of home." He sighed. "I left my big sis, Bree, to cope with it all alone. I barely made the funeral, then went back to fighting."

She squeezed his hands as her eyes crinkled.

Tears gathered in his eyes, and he coughed to remove the lump in his throat. "I felt I'd lost my family, and I kind of had."

She moved closer. "I know that feeling all too well."

He nodded. "But Bree kept at me. Made sure I kept in touch regardless. And when her project renovating Colin's old chapel hit the museums, I had to see what my big sis was up to." He beamed. "I decided to be a better brother and uncle." He blew a laugh. "The twins are hell on earth but so much fun."

Moira smiled. "They are your family, Dom."

He grinned back. "Yeah, family."

She stepped back and released his hands.

When she started to walk away, Dominic grabbed her hand. "Moira, you have family. You have Nubi, the villagers. Your uncle may be gone, but you have people who care for you." He brushed his hand on her cheek. "You have me. I care for you."

Moira nodded but shifted away. Dominic stood there, and for the first time, he had the urge to have a family. One of his own. A home, a wife, and kids. He chuckled. He'd never thought of kids of his own, but here with her—kids felt right.

A man bumped him. He blinked and stood alone in the center of the market. Damn it, he'd lost focus again. What was it with this time that he couldn't keep his military training in check?

Scuffling filled the market as villagers gasped and moved aside. Moira's scream hit him, and her cry was cut short. His gaze roamed the bustle, and he spotted Pierre's thugs dragging Moira away. One limped with a bandaged leg. Well, it seemed Colin's bullet only grazed and didn't strike its mark.

Dominic called out in Arabic as he took off at a run, "New Gourna men, they take Moira!" He caught sight of her white skirt as they rounded the corner and yelled in English, "Moira, hang on. I'm coming."

With his knife unsheathed, he pulled his revolver from under his tunic and rounded the corner to the next aisle in the market, only to find it completely crowded. Was everyone on this aisle?

A short way ahead of him, Dominic recognized three men from the New Gourna group that accompanied them to the market, who stood yelling at the thugs.

One yelled in Arabic, "Thief!" Which drew two officials to them. The other two men from the village wrestled and shoved the thug who held Moira. In the confusion, someone pulled her out of the brute's grasp, and she became enveloped by the crowd.

Dominic's heart skipped as he lost sight of her. He

searched the area. The officials detained the thugs as the dispersing crowd bumped into him, causing Dominic to lose his balance and sidestep. When his head came up, he came face to face with Moira.

The man behind her spoke in Arabic. "The officials detain the men under the charge of thievery. Try to hang on to her better, my friend."

Dominic nodded as he hid his revolver and sheathed his new knife.

Speaking in Arabic, he nodded back. "I will. Thank you, friend."

He took Moira's arm and steered them away to the next aisle. "Are you all right?"

She huffed. "Yes, I am fine. A second attempt in less than twenty-four hours. It's a new record."

Dominic moved them between two stalls. "Moira, I grow concerned. You mentioned that Pierre grew bolder in his attacks, but this is much more aggressive."

Moira shrugged. "It's fine, Dom. I'll be okay. Usually, he loses interest when he gains another of my finds." She glanced away. "With him getting the Divine Family Statue, I thought he'd be gone until it sold," she grumbled. "But it seems he's not satisfied with only taking Evie."

Dominic brushed his hand under her veil to her chin. "Moira, this is dangerous now. Your protection is essential, plus we need you to help us find Pierre and get Evie back." His thumb brushed her lips. He dropped his hand, frustrated with himself for losing focus again. He needed to concentrate on the mission of finding Evie.

Dominic took her hand and stepped back into the market. "It's been a whole day. Where is he?"

They strolled arm in arm through the lane, which was less crowded now.

Moira took a deep breath. "Well, I suspect since he isn't here already, he didn't fly, which leaves only the train. A car can't make it across the desert. No place to fill up with petrol." She peeked at him, grinning. "Pierre wouldn't be caught dead on a camel." She giggled. "And he can't ride them. They hate Pierre more than Colin hates them."

Dominic chuckled. The image of Colin on the camel would be something he would treasure for a long time. "Smart animals."

They walked on a bit as Dominic asked, "So, why the Valley of the Kings?"

Moira eyed a vendor but turned to him. "He might take her to the Temple of Edfu throne room. It's farther away but in this valley."

She glimpsed down. "The room has another Eye of Ra, much larger than the one you came through."

Dominic stopped them. "But why this one? Why not the other?"

Moira glanced up. "This throne room is more powerful than the burial site in Tanis. Plus, Nubi and my workers guard the site in Tanis."

Dominic held her hand. "For what purpose? What does Pierre want?"

Moira snorted. "One thing only—money. But how he's planning to get it, I don't know."

Dominic steered her to the fruit vendor. "Well, think about it and let me know."

****

As Dominic strode alongside, Moira worried about what was to come. Pierre's attacks became more frequent, and her worry for Evie increased by the day. If she felt this way, Brielle must be beside herself. A mother's fear for her daughter was always high, no matter what powers the child held. Brielle's voice echoed in Moira's mind, her plea heartbreaking. Evie was her baby.

She peeked at Dominic beside her. He would stand out no matter where he was. Tall, dashing, and handsome. He towered over most Egyptians, and his muscular frame easily gave him away as a Westerner. Well, at least to her, it did.

The vendor interrupted her thoughts, speaking Arabic. "Dates? They are fresh."

Moira nodded, paid the vendor, then walked off to the side and stared at the Valley of the Kings in the distance. She slid her hand under her veil, popping the fruit into her mouth. As Moira bit down, the sweet date exploded in her mouth. She always liked dates.

The wind ruffled the fabric, and her hand reached under it to touch her lips. The memory of making love to Dominic remained fresh in her mind. Her body still hummed less than a day later. What would living with him be like?

A hand caressed her cheek above the veil, and Dominic whispered next to her ear, "I would give anything to know your mind right now. The expression in your eyes as you touch your lips reminds me of last night." She moved her hand to her bag of dates and gazed down as she blushed. Dominic chuckled in her ear.

He brushed a kiss against her ear. "Your blush tells me all I need to know, Moira. I feel the same."

She turned, gazing at him, and sighed.

He took the bag of dates, popped one into his mouth, and smiled as he chewed the sweet fruit. Moira knew she played with fire, tempting fate. But it was always the same. As soon as things went her way, something would happen, disaster would strike, and she would come out the loser. But for the life of her, she could not stay away from this man. He held her heart in his hands, whether he realized it or not, and there was nothing she could do to stop herself.

She gazed out over the Valley of the Kings, worry new in her mind. This brief glimpse of paradise would end soon. Dominic was from the future. She should know better, but her heart wouldn't listen. Her soul screamed, no!

Dominic cleared his throat. "You should not worry, Moira. It will all work out in the end." He took her hand in his and held it. "It always works out for me. I'll get Evie back and your statue as well."

Moira patted his hand. Of course, it would work out for him. But when it came to Pierre, she was always on the losing end.

Dominic picked up a date and placed it into her mouth under the veil. "It will work out and be just as sweet. Have hope, Moira."

Moira wished so with all her heart. But she knew, just as the sweet fruit in her mouth would sour, so would her life.

Chapter 11

Bree gazed out the train window for hours, seeing the vastness fly by as worry crept into her mind. The clickety-clack of the train's wheels on the rails beat a steady rhythm, unlike her heart. Her fear for Evie ate inside of her to the point there were moments she could think of nothing else. Colin slid into the seat next to her and shifted as he jostled her out of her thoughts.

He snorted and handed her a glass of wine—chardonnay, her favorite. She grinned at him as he placed his arm around her, and she snuggled in the crook of his arm, where she liked to sit and relax.

Today, she didn't feel much like relaxing—thrust back into the 1930s in Egypt. A crazed Frenchman had kidnapped her daughter for her Fae powers, and she sat sipping wine as if they were on a special vacation. She couldn't even take a mouthful of her wine.

"Sip yer wine, Bree. It's yer favorite. Trust me, ye will like it."

She groaned. "I've heard this lecture before."

Her husband grunted as he sipped his wine. "Aye, wife, and ye'll hear it again and again. Drink yer wine. Ye need to relax. She's fine. I feel it in my bones."

She took a sip. It was good.

Colin hummed. "Aye, think of this as a sort of vacation."

Bree sipped her wine again as she glanced around

the first-class cabin. The wood-carved detail on the ceiling and walls was exquisite. The cushioned seats were of fine navy velvet, and the attention to detail rivaled anything from the twenty-first century, which focused on economy instead of luxury.

She sighed. "This is kind of a neat treat, being aboard the Taurus Express. It's the same line that owns the Orient Express and is considered one of the most luxurious lines of the time."

Colin chuckled. "Aye, well, at least we aren't on a train caught in a murder mystery like the book."

Bree licked her lips and took another sip as her husband sighed next to her. "I still can't believe my son stood there straight-faced, lying to the ticket master and got us two first-class cabins without paying." He sipped his wine and grunted. "God help us all when he really figures out what all he can do with power like that."

Bree snorted a laugh. "Too late, husband. He already has."

Colin started to sit up, and Bree placed a hand on his chest. "Before you get all bent out of shape, I have already spoken with him about abusing his powers." She snickered as she took another sip of wine. "I also enlisted Brigid's help."

Colin did growl this time.

Bree patted his chest. He always hated dealing with his Fae. Brigid tormented him at each opportunity she got.

Colin tilted his head to her. "I wince to think what she might consider help. But curiosity has me askin', what did ye have her do?"

Bree barked a laugh. "I asked her to give him a consequence if he abused his powers." Bree giggled and sipped her wine. "She told him parts of his body would fall off if he used his powers wrong or for the wrong thing. I think that's why he asked about using them while we are here. We *are lying*, but it's getting us closer to saving Evie, which is a good cause."

Colin nudged her, and she turned to see his eyebrows near his hairline. "Oh, it's not that bad. I made her promise not to make it happen."

Colin chuckled, trying to stop himself from laughing. "Parts of his body falling off. She didn't suggest…"

Bree giggled and shrugged.

Colin laughed aloud, then heaved a breath. "God, help her. If she makes his pecker fall off, then I will have to kill another Fae." Bree slapped his chest as he laughed. "Well, ye do want grandkids one day. The boy can't produce offspring if Brigid makes his equipment fall off."

Bree sipped her wine. "Grandkids one day, yes. Today, no, and not too soon. They are still young. They must grow up, experience life, and hopefully fall in love."

Colin set his wine down and gathered Bree in his arms. He kissed her ear, and she sighed. Colin took her wine from her, set it beside his, and turned her until she was under him. He caressed her face, and he kissed her deeply.

She tried to sit up. "Colin, I'm worried about Evie."

Colin kissed her again. "Bree, she is fine. Ewan said if anything had gone wrong, he would know it." He kissed her again and spoke low as he caressed her body. "He says it's like that time she fell in the woods, and he knew it when it happened. He said his arm hurt like he had taken the fall, but it was Evie who broke her arm. He was the one who found her by only feeling her. He said he can feel her now, and she's fine."

He kissed her again, and she put her hand on his chest. "Speaking of our son, where is he?"

Colin grinned as he kissed her. "In the gambling car."

She sat up, pushing his chest. "You sent him to the gaming car so he could use his powers?" Colin kissed her as she tried to speak, but he kept kissing her till she stopped.

He spoke between kisses. "No." He kissed her. "I sent him there with some money I got from Dom." He kissed her again. "And told him to see what he can find out about Pierre and his gang." He kissed her as he shifted his hand over her breast, and she moaned. "I told him no powers, and he agreed." He flipped his wife's shirt up and over her head, then kissed her as he lowered her bra. "I told him to keep to his cabin and leave us in peace till the morning."

He took a nipple in his mouth, and Bree sighed. "You, husband, are a wise man."

Colin suckled the other nipple and chuckled. "Aye, wife. That I am." He stripped her bra and pants off in practically one motion, something he had a lot of practice at. He lowered his head to her core. She grabbed his hair and moaned. Colin always liked to taste her, and she enjoyed it, for it drove him crazy. He licked her from bottom to top in one long lick, then repeated it as Bree squirmed in the cramped space of the cabin. Colin sucked her bud, and she nearly screamed out. Colin looked up and smiled, then licked her again as he watched her, leaving her trying not to scream her enjoyment. He toyed with her some more and suddenly sat up.

"Wife, ye are far too attractive today, and I am hungry for ye." He stripped his shirt off, and Bree watched his muscles ripple as he nearly tore his pants off. He was over her, sucking her nipple before she caught her breath. He slid into her so fast she gasped. They both froze and moaned together. Colin moved within her at a pace they both enjoyed time and time again. He growled, and she moaned, for making love to her husband was something that they both loved. He quickened his pace, and soon, they soared for the heavens in ripe ecstasy.

After, Colin gathered her in his arms and covered them with a sheet. They snuggled in the seating, not bothering with converting the cabin into bedding for the night. Bree didn't care. She was content to lie in her husband's arms anywhere.

Colin laughed. "God, woman. Ye drive a man crazy with yer attraction, and then ye kill me with yer hunger for lovin'." He sighed. "I must be getting old." Bree caressed his face but said nothing as she gazed out the train window.

Colin turned her in his arms and used his thumb to tilt her chin till their gazes met. "I can hear yer brain ticking away, Bree. Ye cannot spend all yer time worrying over Evie."

A tear escaped her eye and trailed down her cheek. "She's my baby, Colin, our baby. I miss her and want her in my arms, safe."

Colin wiped the tear away and kissed her wet cheek. "Aye, I know. I worry as well. But we'll get her back. She'll be okay." He kissed her lightly on the lips and rested his forehead against hers, something they did as they worried together. It seemed to make them one as if they could take on the world as long as they were together.

She exhaled, and Colin kissed her. "I love ye, Bree. And I will get our daughter and bring us all home. Safe. I promise."

Bree nodded, and Colin tucked her into his arms. "Have hope, Bree." He held her tight till she drifted off to sleep.

****

Evie beat the door again as the guard kept his back to her. Nothing for dinner and an apple for breakfast—they starved her. Not to mention that she'd not bathed in twenty-four hours or had a change of clothing. The guard finally allowed a bathroom break, but that was after Evie threatened to pee near the entrance, so it'd leak out to him.

She hit the entry again. "Hey, I'm hungry!" The guard's back stayed as Evie slid down the door to the floor. She curled into a ball, hoping for someone—anyone to take pity and give her food. Her body itched, and her mouth had a coating that made her breath—just ew.

The door slid open, and she spilled out onto the floor in the hallway. When she rolled over and glanced up, Pierre folded his arms and glared at her.

She crawled on her knees. "Ye aren't a very hospitable host."

Pierre chuckled. "Oh, pardon. I didn't realize you thought you were a guest."

As she rose, she glared back at him. "Ye aren't a

very good babysitter either. No food, no water." She huffed as she flung her medium-brown wiry hair from her face. "Not even a bath." She thumped his chest. "Yet, here ye stand, perfectly clean, wearing clean clothes."

She lifted her armpit to him. "Have ye smelled me? I stink!"

The guard chuckled as Pierre shifted back, waving his hand before his face. "Well, you do smell, and I can't abide being unclean. The stench of most people in Egypt leaves something...to be desired." He nodded to the guard. "A bath and fresh clothing. Whatever you can find." Evie lowered her arm as Pierre eyed her. "However you can find it. Clothe her properly."

Pierre turned and strode down the hall.

Evie called after him. "Food, I need lunch. And how about dinner!"

Pierre stopped, turned, and strode back. "You better be worth it, girl!" He nudged closer, backing Evie into the wall. "Your magic better work. I want all the riches of Egypt, all of it." He came so close his nose nearly touched hers. "And you will get it for me."

Evie had stood up to some bullies before, but nothing prepared her for a full-fledged crazy man consumed by greed. The look in his eye had her rethinking her games.

She swallowed as Pierre lifted his head, and his eyes traveled down to her top. He grinned. "If you don't give me what I want, I'll take it from you in..." His gaze moved to her pants. "Other ways."

A cold sweat broke out over Evie. The way he leered at her made her stomach turn. She tried to swallow past the lump in her throat as her shaky hand slid down the hall toward the door. Her hand fumbled for the latch, opened it, and she fell into her cabin.

When she looked up, Pierre stood in the doorway. "Take care of my prize. We'll need her later."

The door closed, and a shiver overtook Evie.

A while later, Evie sat running her fingers through her wet hair. The bath was nothing more than a bowl with a jug of water, a bar of soap, and a towel. She'd had what Mrs. A called a "whore's bath" and used the remaining water to wash her hair.

The clothing was interesting—all white and soft linen—like the people she'd seen here. Something so lightweight Evie didn't feel like she wore much, but she had on pants, a skirt, and a tunic of sorts. There was a veil and a hat thingy, but Evie opted not to put them on. The guard delivered a meal of spiced beef with flatbread, reminding her of gyros.

As she sat, she took inventory of her skills and tried to formulate a plan for wherever Mr. P would take her. She needed to be ready. The rock splitting had served its purpose, so she wasn't sure how or if she'd use that again. She didn't want to use the glowing ball unless she needed her dream boy. A Fae, for sure. She wasn't certain where he came from, but she'd save him for real emergencies. The portal power was practically unknown to her. Only recently had she begun working on her stronger powers. She needed to work on the ability to control them, so when she used them, they worked to her advantage.

What else? Sometimes, if she was close to someone she knew well, she could send a mental message, like Ewan. But not always. There was the ability to sense her brother, although his power was stronger than hers. His power centered on minds, and hers centered on emotions—like the powers surrounding people. She sat and thought about it more, but nothing came to mind.

The Stone of Hope. That was a puzzle, for sure. Why were she and Ewan here? The Fae usually tasked the adults with finding the stones, not mere kids.

The quote. "But those who have hope will renew their strength. They will run and not grow weary; they will walk and not be faint; they will soar like wings on eagles."

What did it mean, and how did it tell how to find the stone? She ticked off her fingers. The Stone of Love was in a necklace. The Stone of Fear was in a cross, but the fable wasn't about the stone at all. The Stone of Lust, Balor, the evil Fae King, had. Brigid said the fables told all, but what did arguing brothers have to do with the Stone of Hope?

A clean body and a full stomach had her drifting to sleep. As she drifted off, she thought, *I need to be ready*.

****

Dominic stood drinking spiced tea as the villagers conversed around him. The village had planned a feast for this evening. In the village center was a large rock, inside of which an Egyptian cross of fine silver sat. About three feet in height, the thing had to be worth a small fortune. Obviously, it was important to them, yet they left it unguarded.

Moira took a little longer to get ready this evening. The villager beside him glanced over his shoulder and stood taller. Dominic turned, and Moira approached. Her hair flowed loose, and her gown twinkled in the light. Moira had not wasted her extra time.

Silver accents decorated her black dress that accentuated her auburn hair, and the sheer hijab perfectly set off the tanned hazelnut of her skin. When Dominic turned her way, his eyes focused on her lips, visible under the gauzy fabric of her veil, reminding him of her kisses from last night.

He put his arm around her when she came beside him and spoke lowly, "You look lovely this evening." Fresh jasmine wafted to him, her favored scent now imprinted in his mind as Moira.

Moira blushed. "You as well."

Mamduh called out. "Ahh, our guest of honor has arrived." He waved to the front, where tables sat out under the starry night, weighed down with large servings of various dishes. He handed Moira tea and toasted the group. "To Miss Moira, our provider, and the keeper of the Gods' treasures. The Gods smile upon you, my dear, as we honor you."

Pride swelled in Dominic for Moira. Her accomplishments and care for these people were evident in the people's expressions as they saluted her.

Mamduh signaled them to serve first, and the rest of the village soon followed. As they sat and ate, many stopped by congratulating Moira or thanking her for her service to the town. She should be honored.

He leaned in and whispered, "Moira, you are a treasure and should be very proud." She blushed.

Dominic escorted her to the head table, which sat before the rest. Mamduh waved for them to sit. When they did, the village sat in unison, and people happily passed the feast around for everyone to share. Spiced beef accompanied with steamed vegetables and flatbread made for a hearty meal. Spiced tea and mulled wine made the meal a banquet for all. Dominic filled his plate and grinned at her as they ate in companionable silence.

After the village had their fill of food, Mamduh stood and set his bowl aside.

He approached Dominic and Moira, nodding to Dominic. "You are not aware of the village's purpose. Our story I will share for our newcomer, Moira's warrior." He turned and waved his hands, forming a circle. "Our village's pride and joy." He brought them together and held them tight. "The Ankh or key of life, a symbol of life itself." The village people brought their hands together and bowed their heads as if praying.

Moira grinned, warming up to the explanation of Mamduh's purpose in life—to protect the Ankh. "The Ankh has a cross shape, but with a teardrop-shaped loop in place of a vertical upper bar."

Dominic muttered, "I thought I recognized the symbol from my tour in Saudi."

Mamduh walked in the circle before the villagers, making eye contact with each. "We believe life is a force that circulates throughout the world." His single hand waved above him. "Individual living things, including humans, are demonstrations of this force and fundamentally tied to it."

Moira sat back, content to listen to Mamduh tell his duty and purpose for likely the hundredth time. Each telling grew increasingly animated with each new guest he had the opportunity to share it with.

He waved his hands in a circle, then each up and down opposite each other. "Life came into existence at the world's creation, and the rising and setting of the sun are the creation that maintained and renewed life in the cosmos." His hand rose to the sky, the orange rays of the setting sun adding to the dramatic telling of his story. "The Gods made the renewal of life come through water. Each year, we have restored life from the Nile. It takes life when it rises angry but gives life when it recedes, making the land bountiful." Moira's eye caught Dominic's, and he winked at her.

Mamduh crossed to the rock with the Ankh. "The Gods who governed these natural cycles sustained life. Therefore, the Ankh represents their life-giving power. When humans die, these natural cycles renew their lives in the same manner. The pharaoh represented Egypt as a whole, so by giving the sign to him, the Gods granted life to the entire nation."

Mamduh waved his hand over the villagers. "The Gods gave the village the Ankh, representing the power to bestow life. We must protect it for the Gods and the pharaohs. Kept here, it has sustained our village and protected us as we have protected the symbol for the Gods. It is most sacred to us."

Dominic nodded. "A noble duty for a noble man. Your village is nice. I thank you for your hospitality."

He stood and took Moira's hand. "A stroll?" She nodded. A walk in the sunset would be nice. They wandered a bit hand in hand. They came to the cliff overlooking the Valley of the Kings.

****

Dominic stood staring at the setting sun over the Valley of the Kings. Moira walked up next to him, looking at the sight before them. There was something different about the sunset in the desert than any other place in the world.

She glanced his way and caught him staring at her with a smile.

She turned to him. "What are you smiling at?"

Dominic stepped closer to her and touched her cheek. "Just looking at how beautiful you are in the setting sunlight. It's like you are bathed in gold, glittering just for me."

Moira blushed and looked down. "I am certain it is the light playing tricks on your eyes. I am usually covered in dirt from head to toe and in need of a good bath."

Dominic unhooked the face covering, allowing it to drop, exposing her face from the garb they needed to disguise themselves. "You are a unique woman, Moira. I don't think you realize just how extraordinary you are." He bent and kissed her lips lightly.

She returned his kiss and exhaled as he lifted his head till their faces were a mere breath apart. "Such modern a woman caught in a time like this. It's as if you aren't meant to be here."

Moira stifled a laugh. "Sometimes I feel like I'm not meant to be here."

Dominic kissed her again, trailed kisses along her cheek to her ear, and said, "I wish, I wish…" He kissed her ear. "I wish you could come with me. I want to be with you, Moira. I want to be with you always."

He kissed her neck, and she sighed. "I wish that as well, but this. It's not meant to be."

Dominic lifted his head and kissed her lips deeply. He raised his head and gazed into her eyes. She tilted her head and returned his stare.

"Come with me, Moira. When we finally get through this, come to the future to be with me."

Moira barked a laugh. "Dom, I can't do that. I don't even know how."

Dominic took her hands in his. "It's like walking down the street. You just walk through the portal. There's a bit of a headache after, but it fades."

Moira dropped his hands and turned away, looking at the valley. "I am certain there is more to it than walking through a hole." She glanced over her shoulder. "I have responsibilities here, Dom. I can't just up and leave them. What of my digs? What of Nubi and the villagers? I can't leave them to the fate of Pierre. He would enslave them, and the digs are their main source of income."

Dominic took her by the shoulder, turning her to face him. "I want to be with you." He breathed, glimpsed away, and turned back to her. "What if something happened to you and I wasn't here? What if I wasn't here to help you, to save you?" He shook her shoulders with the last of his speech.

She studied his face as he spoke. The intensity of his gaze and the crinkle of his eyes spoke of much more than mere concern.

"You know something. You know something of the future. Of my future."

Dominic took her into his arms and held her there for a moment. "Please come with me, Moira."

God, what she wouldn't give to be with him. So tempting—go away, start anew. Like a fairy tale, but it was that, a tale.

She broke out of his embrace. "I can't come with you. Whatever fate has in store for me, that will be my future. With or without you."

She started to walk away, but Dominic grabbed her

and embraced her. He kissed her hard and deeply as if he poured all his emotions into this passionate kiss. She moaned, and he tilted his head to gain better access to her mouth, her soul.

He lifted his head briefly. "I will not let you go. Not now and not ever, Moira." He lifted her into his arms, turned, and entered their hut. He lowered her to stand before him and kissed her again. He was so soft, so sweet, her warrior.

Dominic gently removed her hijab, and his gaze dropped as her mass of auburn curls tumbled free. He ran both hands through them and pulled the waterfall of curls to one side.

He kissed her ear lightly, and she giggled at the contact. He trailed kisses down her neck as he undid the buttons on her tunic. The fabric gradually fell off her shoulders, exposing her creamy skin, and Dominic's kisses traveled to her shoulder, then lower to her breast. The tunic fell to the floor, and she sighed as he took a nipple into his mouth and suckled. She ran her hands through his hair and moaned as he licked her nipple.

She reached for his tunic, and he removed it in one motion. Tossing it aside as he kicked off his boots, he grabbed her and rubbed his bare chest against hers as she dropped her head back. As he kissed down her chest, he stripped her underwear down, stopping at her boots. He knelt before her like before carefully untying and removing one boot at a time. She helped as he blew on her curls, sending chills through her. As he rose, he picked her up, turned, and laid her on the bed. He stood over her, looking at her. She blushed and tried to cover herself.

He grabbed her hands and kissed them both. "No,

you are beautiful, and I want to see you. I want to see your beauty, Moira."

He lay beside her and took her into his arms as he kissed her.

She ran her hand over his chest and moaned. "I like your muscles, and the hair tickles me, makes me tingle."

Dominic smiled as her hand slid down the front of his body and cupped his arousal through his pants. He shifted and lay on his back, allowing her the chance to explore his body. She followed his lead and sat up on her elbow, massaging him. She tugged on his pants, and he pulled them down, then sat up and took them off. Dominic lay back down, allowing her to look her fill. She tilted her head and studied his body. His shaft jumped as her eyes traveled down. He gazed into her face. She had such a wondering look as she took in his body.

She ran her fingers down his chest, took his rod into her hand, and stroked it once. He closed his eyes and moaned.

She softly said, "You like that?"

He opened his eyes. "Very much. Especially since it's you doing it."

She ran her hand up and down again, and his hips bucked. His hand came up behind her head, and he brought her mouth to his and kissed her deeply as she continued her torture of his body. Their tongues danced, and he moaned as she continued to stroke him. His other hand took her breast, and he squeezed it. Dom grabbed her and settled her astride him.

"You keep touching me like that, and this will be over before you satisfy your desires." He kissed her, and he guided her to slide her slit over his shaft. She was already wet, and he hadn't even touched her yet.

"Moira, I want you so much it hurts." He slid himself over her again, and this time, she tilted her hips to take him inside of her. He moaned as he slowly filled her, and when he reached his hilt, she sat up and threw her head back with one long groan. Dominic grabbed her hips as if to anchor himself as she began to rock over his shaft. Her hands gripped his wrists as if she needed something to hold on to, and Dominic helped show her how to ride him.

She started slowly but soon quickened her pace as she repeatedly threw her head to the side and the back with each thrust and moan. He guided her over him as she rocked back and forth, her head shifting with the movement. Her hair flew over one shoulder and then the other. She was so beautiful. With a thrust into her, she cried out his name. Unable to stand it anymore, he had to have control. Dominic flipped her onto her back and drove into her over and over. She grabbed his shoulders as he kissed her. He thrust into her again and arched as he cried out her name, pouring all his heart into her.

Dominic collapsed on her and buried his face in her neck, panting from his efforts. He lifted his head and took her face between his hands, still connected. Dominic kissed her lightly on the lips and moved within her, his arousal still with him. He gazed into her eyes as she gazed back. "Moira, I love you."

She swallowed. "Dom, I…" She paused when he shifted.

Dominic kissed her, then lifted his head. "You don't have to say anything. I just wanted you to know how I feel." He slowly slid out of her and rolled to her side, taking her with him. "No matter what, Moira, I wanted you to know how I felt about you."

She exhaled and rested her head against his chest. Her warrior loved her.

He kissed the top of her head. "You don't have to worry, Moira. We'll deal with tomorrow when it comes. But for now, I just want to hold you."

Chapter 12

Colin sat with Bree in the train's dining car as she sipped her favorite rich, dark coffee, and he tried the Egyptian tea. The vivid flavors of the new brew grew on him the more he drank it.

Ewan slid into the seat beside him. As Colin took another sip, he examined his son, who wore the same clothes as yesterday. His ruffled look told him he hadn't bothered to brush his hair, like always. Colin chuckled—typical teenager. Ewan spent energy getting them all transportation, a change of clothes, and essentials to wash and groom but didn't bother to use them himself.

Bree smirked. "Good morning, slug-a-bug."

Ewan grunted and lifted the pot of coffee, pouring himself a cup. Bree raised her eyebrows and eyed him as Ewan added cream and sugar, two spoonsful to his cup.

When he sipped it, he lifted his gaze to his parents. "Coffee tastes awful, but I need it."

He sipped again and set the cup down. "I was up late. People had a lot to say about Frenchie man." The car rocked a little as the wheels clicked on the rails.

Colin growled, adjusting his seat. "Go on."

Ewan took a roll and bit into it as he spoke around the bread. "Pierre is a right sneaky bastard."

Bree set her cup down, clattering the china.

"Language, Ewan."

Ewan sipped more coffee and swallowed the mixture of liquid and bread. "Ye sound like Uncle Dom."

Colin poured Ewan more coffee. "Explain and leave nothing out." His eyes slid to his wife. "Language and all." He needed all the information they could get, and it seemed his crafty son would deliver.

Bree lifted her shoulder as she stuck her tongue out at him, reminding him of all the things she did with it last night. He grinned as he turned to their son, nodding for him to continue.

Ewan sat up, seeming ready to give his report. "It's all true. The slave labor, the stealing of Moira's digs, his bribing the government. The people of Egypt hate him."

Colin exchanged a look with Bree. So Pierre was a bad guy. He reached his hand out to hers, and they grasped each other. Colin squeezed once as he always did, giving her reassurance all would be well. She worried for Evie, but their otherworldly daughter always had a way of coming out on top.

Ewan's gaze went from his hands to his mother's face, then his da's. "She's fine. I can still feel her. That means she's not too far."

Bree patted her son's hand. "Thank you, Ewan."

Colin tapped the table. "What else?"

Ewan set his cup down. "The Egyptians are a pretty superstitious lot, Da. They claim Frenchie man steals from the Gods, sells sacred items to become rich, and the Gods allow it." He bit into his breakfast roll, speaking around it again. "They say his end is coming, and the Gods will see to it."

Colin grumbled, "Damn straight, his end is coming."

Ewan set the roll down. "One man pulled me aside. He said the people who looked for the magic stone brought hope to the people of Egypt." Ewan glanced at Bree and then back at him.

Bree gasped. "A magic stone? Colin, could it be something related to the Stone of Hope?"

Colin shook his head. "Ewan, anything about brothers or siblings arguing?"

Ewan shook his head as the waiter set the check on the table.

His son pulled a wad of bills from his pocket. "Here, Da, some money to pay for it."

Colin sat back waving at the bills. "And where did this bounty come from?"

Ewan counted out the pound notes. "Well, ye can't send me gambling and not expect me to play the part, Da!"

****

"Where is this again?" Evie asked as Pierre escorted her toward a large building, square with large shapes of people carved into the front. The doorway was equally large.

"Keep walking forward, *fille girl*. This is the Temple of Edfu. The temple worshipping Horace." As they passed them in the hallway, Evie tried studying the hieroglyphics, but Pierre wouldn't allow her to stop.

It was the following afternoon, and Pierre had not permitted them to rest. He had all his equipment ready for a campsite in the Valley of the Kings in an hour. They'd traveled by cars and trucks filled with more stuff than Evie could imagine was needed. He seemed ready to excavate an entire pyramid with so many men and so much equipment.

He led her through the central entry into an inner courtyard with large pillars taller than Dunstaffnage Castle. She paused and turned, gazing at them, but Pierre pulled her along.

At the next doorway, a black statue of an eagle stood to the left. The eagle! The quote ran through her mind. "But those who have hope will renew their strength. They will run and not grow weary; they will walk and not be faint; they will soar like wings on eagles."

Evie stopped. "Hey, what's with the eagle statue?"

Pierre grabbed her hand and pulled her into the next doorway. "It's Horus as an eagle. This way, girl."

She recalled the story Moira had told them the first night they'd arrived in the past, the Divine Family story. Horus was the son and eventual king and ruler of Egypt. She didn't understand why Mr. P would go to the trouble to drag her across Egypt to another tomb underground when the portal was back at the other vault. The one Moira worked in. Evie sighed. She wanted her parents, and she wanted to go home.

She entered a large room that they'd cleared of rubble and artifacts. Energy buzzed in the room, making Evie pause. They stood on a large wooden platform that rose over the throne room. As she glanced up, the ceiling was a high arch. At the far end of the room sat a large gold throne beneath the stand. Evie allowed her gaze to travel up the wall behind it. She gasped. Embedded in the wall was a golden Eye of Ra twice as large as the one used before as a portal. As her stare settled upon the eye, she felt the energy pull at her and took a step back.

Bumping into Pierre, he took hold of her shoulders. "*Magnifique, magnificent*, isn't it, girl?"

She shrugged out of his arms and turned to face him. She had to keep her eyes away from the golden artifact so the portal wouldn't open. She needed to convince Pierre there was nothing she could do here. If not, who knew what might happen?

She folded her arms. "It's just another eye. It doesn't mean it's a portal. I am certain there are many just like this all over Egypt."

Pierre smirked at her. "Many painted on walls, *oui*, girl. But this is the only one made of gold but inlaid into the wall. If the other was a portal, then it stands to reason this one will be as well."

He spun her so quickly she tripped on her own two feet, and had Pierre not been holding her, she would have fallen forward off the platform. She kept her gaze on the ground, anywhere but the eye.

Mr. P squeezed her. "Open it, girl. I need power. The power of the portal to bring me all the riches of Egypt."

She pulled sideways out of his embrace, facing him. "It doesn't work that way. It doesn't have an on-and-off switch."

Pierre grabbed her arm hard as she cried out. "*Ouvre-le. Open it.* The portal, now!"

Evie needed to figure out something to pacify him and make it seem like she tried to open the portal but couldn't. The ball of light would impress him, but for how long? It was all she had. The rock trick was old news now.

She gathered her energy and hoped this would

work, anything to keep Mr. P happy. Evie knew she couldn't control the portal alone and didn't want to try—anything to stop the portal from opening.

She flicked her wrist like the Fae boy had shown her, and nothing happened. She took a deep breath and tried again, and a small spatter of energy pulsed through her, but then nothing.

Evie closed her eyes and focused on the Fae boy, the kiss, and how it made her feel. Focusing, with her eyes still closed, she flicked her wrist again. Warmth flooded her hand, and all her emotions and feelings for the Fae boy returned full force.

Pierre gasped. Evie slowly opened her eyes, and the ball of light sat in her palm. She peeked at the eye, and it began to turn. She quickly closed her eyes and made a few grunting noises to make it seem like she tried to open the portal.

Pierre grabbed her. "Girl, open the portal." When he touched her, she lost focus, and the light disappeared.

She smirked inwardly. Mr. P had caused her to lose concentration, and she could easily blame him. "Ye can't touch me. Ye broke the contact." She sighed loudly for effect. "Now, I'll never be able to open the eye."

Pierre roared, grabbed her, and yanked her to him. He turned her hard and forced her to face the eye. Pierre held a knife to her cheek, the point pressing on her soft skin.

He leaned down and spoke in her ear, "You will stop playing games with me." He slid the knife down her cheek and pressed it near the jawline, making a small slice.

Evie flinched and whimpered as Pierre hissed in her ear. "You will open the eye now, or I will begin to cut."

Evie's breath hitched, but she said in a high, small voice, "If ye hurt me, I have no power."

Pierre laughed. "I am beginning to see your games, girl. You will stop now."

The boy of her dreams strode into her line of sight. He nodded and turned to Ra's Eye, raising his hands. A wind howled through the chamber, swirling around them. The boy lounged as if holding the force of the eye back as the portal spun fast.

Evie cried out, "No!"

Pierre loosened his hold on her and cried out, "*Oui!*"

The portal spun, but there was no picture or movie inside. It wasn't open, only started.

The boy glanced over his shoulder at Evie, his arms still raised. His voice came to her mind. *~Tell him to release ye, and ye will bring the mummy through the portal. Tell him ye will give him all that he wants, all he desires…the power of the pharaoh to gain his riches. But he must leave ye alone. He can never hurt ye again. ~*

Evie shook her head, but the boy's voice yelled. *~Do it, Evie. It will keep you safe from harm. ~*

Evie took a deep breath and yelled, "I can bring the mummy through the portal. Ye will control him, and he can give ye all the riches of Egypt."

Pierre screamed, "*Oui*, do it, girl."

She stepped away from him. "There is a price for yer prize—my safety. If ye hurt me in any way, I will take the power away from yer dead man."

Pierre stood staring at the eye. In the center, the mummy stood staring back.

Pierre grinned and growled, "Anything, girl."

The boy's voice came to her. *~So be it. All the power and all the evil will be his. In the end, it will be his doom. ~*

The youth moved, one hand shoved toward them, sending them back, and with the other, he sent a shockwave into the portal as the mummy came through headfirst, landing at Evie's feet.

The wind stopped. When Evie looked up, the boy had vanished. She turned to Pierre, who glared at the corpse on the floor. Evie took a step back and then another. The dead body groaned and slowly rose to his feet. He advanced toward Evie as she backed up quickly. The mummy followed, only to fall in a heap on the floor.

Pierre cried out. "What is wrong with him?"

Evie was against the far wall from the eye and the throne. "The eye seems to power him. He cannot get too far from it."

Pierre pointed at the corpse. "Well, move him."

Evie fisted her hands at her side. "He's too big. I can't."

Pierre grunted and stepped toward the dead body, bent and dragged him closer to the throne. As Pierre drew closer to the throne, the corpse came to life. Pierre bowed, motioning to the throne, and the mummy sat and nodded.

Pierre kneeled and spoke in Arabic.

The Fae boy's voice whispered the translation in her head, nearly making her jump out of her skin. *~I require yer powers, Pharaoh. Which king are ye? ~* She must have jolted because Pierre glanced her way. She froze, staring at the dead man in wraps, praying she hadn't given herself up.

The corpse nodded, replying in Arabic in a deep, echoing voice.

The boy repeated it for her. *~I am Psusennes I, Pharaoh of high Egypt. ~*

Pierre approached the mummy as he spoke lowly.

The boy repeated the translation. *~In a village near here, there is a cross, an ankh, the key of life. ~*

He added. *~Crap, now I know what Frenchie is after. ~*

The dead man nodded, speaking in Arabic.

The boy spoke. *~The key of the Nile. With it, I can have eternal life. ~* The boy snorted. *~He wants eternal life for the mummy. ~*

Pierre smiled as he replied.

~Yes, and the price for it. Ye shall give me all the riches of Egypt. ~ The translation had Evie gasping, but she covered her mouth.

The corpse nodded.

Pierre chuckled as he spoke again.

The translation came. *~Also, a woman. Moira White in the village, my woman. Bring her to me. Damn, they go after Moira, that old Frenchie wants her for himself. ~*

The mummy chanted over and over in Arabic as a single translation came to her. *~Rise, my army, rise! ~*

Moans filled the chamber. Groups of marching feet filled the hallway. Evie scanned the exit of the room. A figure on the wall started to move. Then, it grew from the wall and became whole. When she realized he was a hieroglyphic come to life, she screamed. Five filled the chamber, all made from sand, wearing the same clothing as in the drawings.

Evie backed up, and Pierre caught her, holding on to her arm. "Don't leave now, Evie. The fun's just getting started."

Evie struggled in his arms. "What's happening?"

Pierre laughed. "He's called forth the army of the dead, Psusennes' army, to serve me."

The mummy spoke to his generals of the dead, but the boy's translation did not come. Did he leave her? Was she all alone? She needed someone, anyone on her side.

The five bowed to their leader and exited the chamber.

Evie whispered, "What now? Why are they leaving?"

Pierre followed, dragging Evie, who tugged his arm. "Ye promised not to hurt me."

Pierre dropped her arm. "Then come along. See the army of the dead." He chuckled as he led Evie out into the valley.

When she exited the tunnel, she gasped as she gazed upon hundreds of sandmen, like the five in the chamber. They swirled into the wind and disappeared.

Evie gasped. "Oh, God. What have I done?"

Chapter 13

Moira sat with Dominic, enjoying lunch with some villagers. The villagers had a large cone of pressed lamb and rotated it over a flame, cooking it evenly. Once browned, they sliced off pieces and mixed them in a skillet with chopped tomato, onion, and parsley before being rolled into a large disc of flatbread. Moira's mouth watered. She loved *shawarma*.

Dominic sat and studied his flatbread filled with spiced meat and vegetables. "It looks like a gyro just missing the tzatziki sauce. Same as the *shawarma* I had in Saudi on a military tour," Dominic spoke between bites. "It's quite tasty."

Moira grinned as she ate hers. "Well, it is *shawarma* here as well. The kabobs are good as well. But baklava is my favorite."

Dominic nodded. "Baklava—I know what that is. Nuts and honey with pastry layered in sweet goodness."

Moira smiled as Dominic winked at her. They ate in silence, finishing their meal. Moira moved to take the plates and cups as Dominic cleaned his hands.

After thanking the villagers, they walked on into the village. Moira waited for Pierre to arrive, and her concern for Evie put her on edge. She needed to share all she figured out with Dominic.

She turned to him. "Pierre's headed to the Valley of the Kings." She sighed. "He stole a whole dig from me there years ago. It was to be my greatest find. The first for a woman to discover and solidify my place in archeological history. It was another son of Ramesses II."

She shivered recalling that day. His threats, his touch.

Dominic touched her arm, bringing her out of the memory. "Tell me of it."

Moira turned, tears in her eyes as she shook her head. "All those years as my uncle's partner, and Pierre wanted me. Even when I was a young teen, he lusted for me." She shuddered, and Dominic took her into his arms. She found such comfort there, from this warrior of hers from a future time.

They stood there staring at the village as Moira muttered, "I suspected but didn't know for sure till that day. Pierre killed my uncle. While I wasn't there to witness it, he practically admitted it."

Dominic held her and kissed her head. "I'm sorry. Your uncle was a great man. A loss for the Egyptologist community." Pierre could be cruel, especially when he didn't get all he wanted. And with Evie in his custody...

She shivered and stepped out of Dominic's embrace. "I worry for Evie being in Pierre's possession." She glanced at him.

Dominic's expression grew hard. "Moira, he must keep Evie safe. She holds the powers he needs. Tell me what you know. Let us talk this through."

She nodded, the practical part of her mind taking over. Her knowledge of Egypt flowed easily, reducing her fears and anxiety.

She took a calming breath. "The mummy that came

to life, he's Psusennes I, Pharaoh of high Egypt."

She took his hand, and they walked to the cliff's edge overlooking the Valley of the Kings. "Pierre's headed to the Valley of the High Kings." Her hand waved over the valley before them. "He might take her to the throne room of the Temple of Edfu. It's farther away but in this valley."

She gazed out over the valley. "The room has another Eye of Ra, much larger than the one you came through." She glanced back at him. "I fear it may be another portal."

Dominic nodded. "You mentioned that before. Evie said the eye called her. She'd visited it many times."

Moira tilted her head. "Visited, how?"

Dominic grinned. "Ah, you'll like this. The Eye of Ra from your dig sits in a museum in Florida, the United States, in the future. Many visit it regularly, and the exhibit travels the world."

Moira smiled. "In a museum. That's great. It's why I work so hard. To share all this with the world."

Dominic patted her hand. "Yes, well. The eye Evie must power, and it spins. Then we see what's on the other side, before the other eye."

Moira blushed. "That's how you saw me? Before?"

Dominic nodded, then cleared his throat. "The portals are connections between the world of Fae and humans. The one we know of is a time portal. Evie only stumbled upon this one."

He turned and gazed over the valley. "Something must have gone wrong. It pulled us through after Evie lost control." His gaze came back to her. His eyes crinkled in concern. "When the shaft of light came out of the portal, it hit the mummy, and I suspect that's what brought him to life." Portals and time travel again. She focused, trying to wrap her mind around all Dominic shared.

He took her hands in his. "Moira, the light that hit a dead man, bringing him to life. We face something much more powerful and evil than just Pierre." He took a deep breath. "It's evil Fae power."

She turned. "Why tell me all this?"

Dominic nodded. "The kids mentioned the quotes from your Divine Family story matched some from the *Fae Fable Book*. It's the book given to the MacDougalls that tells the fate of the lost magic Fae stones. They mentioned it was the story of the Stone of Hope. Evie said it was a long rectangular green stone but broken in half. It means we hunt a Fae stone lost in space and time. Human will and emotion power the stones. Bree mentioned it was like collecting and channeling all your emotions into one focus, and the stone will do as you command."

Moira's mind digested all this. Magic stones and time travel, but what did any of this have to do with Egypt or her?

Dominic squeezed her hands, bringing her attention back to him. "We must recover the Stone of Hope, but we don't know where it is. Usually, the fable tells us. Colin had a brief chance to fill me in, but I'm still confused between the Fae fable story of brothers arguing and yours about the Divine Family and how they connect to tell us where the stone is."

She glanced down, her mind quickly recalling the quotes. "Bree mentioned the curse matched a quote. Is that what you refer to?"

Dominic blinked. "Yes, the same as the curse for the mummy."

He caressed her face. "Moira, I need your help. Your knowledge of Egypt. Of what Pierre may plan and do. Your expertise will help. So, whatever you can share, I need to know."

The wind picked up and swirled as it gained in strength. Some villagers ran for cover in their homes, but Moira stood beside Dom, wondering what was happening. Sandstorms didn't come this time of year.

Dominic stood and glanced around. "Prepare yourself, Moira. Swirling wind with no one else around only means a Fae power gathers. But who and what this time? The twins aren't anywhere nearby. Where is this power coming from, and what will it bring?"

Streams of sand dropped from the sky in groups. As it hit the earth, it materialized into men.

Moira spoke in awe. "Are those men? They appear to be hieroglyphics."

It wasn't until one swiped his sword at Dominic that they moved, progressing like an army.

Dominic grabbed Moira's hand and made a run for their hut. "It's not a movie, darling. These move and are armed."

Moira yelled over the chaos, "It's the mummy! Pierre had summoned the pharaoh and his powers."

Dominic hit one of the men. It dissolved into the dirt at his feet and regenerated into a figure again as Dom pulled Moira behind him. "What the hell are these?"

Moira and Dominic ducked as another figure tried to grab them. "Psusennes I was buried with hundreds of *ushabtis*, figurines of servants that would magically come to life and serve the pharaoh in the next world."

Dominic kicked the figure, and he fell into a pile of brown dirt. Dominic dragged her farther away from the fighting.

As they ran past the main square in the center of the village, the village leader, Mamduh, ran up to her. "The Ankh, they have taken it. Our sacred symbol of life. The army of the dead has taken the cross." The Ankh, the key to life, was gone.

Moira stopped. "Why would they take that?"

Mamduh was struck from behind and fell at her feet.

Dominic grabbed her hand, pulling her along. "No time for chitchat."

They cleared the next turn and made it into their hut. Dominic slammed the door and dug through his bag, pulling out the revolver. He grabbed the rifle from beside the bed and fastened an ammunition belt over his tunic.

Her warrior turned to her, fully armed, ready to fight the army alone. "I need some answers, Moira. You need to tell me what all this means so I'll know how to fight this."

She quickly ran the facts through her mind, speaking as they came. "An army of the dead. I've never heard of one coming to life, but that must be what this is."

She paced, and Dominic peeked out the flap over the window. "The fighting has stayed mostly within the village square, but I'm uncertain it will remain there."

He dropped the flap. "Can I kill them?"

Moira barked a laugh. "How would I know? Based upon what I have seen today, I don't think so." She paced again. "Why the Ankh? Why take that?" She snapped her fingers. "That's it. It is known as *the key of the Nile*, the union between Osiris and Isis. The Ankh represents eternal life."

Dominic snapped his gaze to hers. "Does that mean what I think it means?"

Moira bit her lip. "The pharaoh plans to use it for eternal life, to become immortal."

Dominic cursed under his breath. "Damn, I could use Colin right now."

Moira kept pacing as she spoke. "Oh, I knew he would try to take her to the throne room of the Temple of Edfu. Pierre plans to use the mummy to control the world, and he's used Evie to bring the mummy here. I had counted on the villagers to alert us when he arrived." She peeked at Dominic and shrugged. "Apparently, that hasn't worked. He's already here."

The hut's door burst open, and two members of the dead army stood there. Dominic shot one, and he fell as dirt to the floor.

Another two came through the door. The first went straight for Moira, grabbing her as she screamed, "Dom!"

One swiped his sword at Dominic, who ducked, moving away from the door. "Moira, I can't shoot. I might hit you."

She struggled as they dragged her toward the door. "Dom, Dom. Do something!"

Dominic lunged for her. Another brown figure appeared and swiped his sword, cutting Dominic's arm. He bellowed in pain as he grabbed his arm.

The two holding her dragged her out of the hut and through the open door. As they pulled her away, she saw them attacking Dominic.

Dominic lunged again, and two more fighters grabbed him, holding each arm as another stepped forward, punching him in the face once, and again. His head fell forward as he was hit in the stomach twice more. His body jolted from the impact.

Moira screamed, and he glanced up. Through the doorway, their eyes connected. As the members of the dead army held Dominic up, they punched him again.

The sandmen holding her stopped. The wind whistled loudly. The Earth tilted as she screamed, "Dominic, I love you."

Her last vision of him was the fighters releasing him as he fell face-first to the ground.

Chapter 14

Colin grunted. "I cannot believe ye allowed Pierre to take Moira. Now we not only have Evie to worry about but now Moira."

Colin glared at Dominic, who scowled back at his brother-in-law while sporting a bloodied nose and swollen eye, thanks to members of the army of the dead. "It wasn't just Pierre. They were an army of the dead. Large sandmen you can't kill. It's not like I stood there, pointed to her, and said, 'Here she is, boys!' "

Dominic patted a cold cloth to his eye. Colin, Bree, and Ewan had arrived by the Taurus Express train earlier in the day and gathered to plan how to rescue Evie and Moira.

Bree placed her hand on Colin's arm. "Colin, we need to focus on what Mamduh is telling us. There has to be something we can do to stop the ceremony and rescue Evie and Moira."

As they all sat around the lantern inside Moira's hut, Mamduh, the village leader, explained the significance of the throne room and the ritual he suspected Pierre had planned with the mummy. "The temple is built at the location of the fight between Horus and Seth, where Horus defeated Seth to rule the kingdoms. It leads into the throne room, or as some called it, the offering room. Inside are the twelve papyrus columns that symbolize the concept of

Amduat, the nightly journey of the sun God Ra through the twelve regions of the netherworld. Each takes an hour."

Ewan spoke from beside his mother. "Twelve worlds. That's a long ritual. Will we have to be there for hours, and how would we stay hidden from Pierre during that time?"

Bree sat up straighter. "Let's let Mamduh tell us what he can." She glared at her husband. "Without interruption. There's something here. We have to find it." She nodded to Mamduh to continue.

"This is why Pierre chose this temple, the Amduat. Many believe that if the dead followed this path through the netherworld, the dead would become undead and immortal. The Ankh shall carry the mummy to the netherworld to permit him inside each world so he may complete the journey, thus completing the ritual, becoming rejuvenated, gaining immortality, with the reward of Egypt's riches. If you break the ritual, then chaos shall ensue and death to all around."

Dominic set the cloth aside and sighed heavily. "Okay, so how do we break the ritual? There has to be a way to break it."

Mamduh sputtered. "It is not wise to break the ritual. Death will come *to all* around. That will include you and your friends." He glanced around him and spoke with authority. "Miss Moira has been a friend to us for many years. I do not wish anything to happen to her. While I want her freed, I don't want her death as the result of tempting the wrath of the Gods."

Bree's gaze traveled between them all and then to Mamduh. "Explain the ritual, and we shall see what we can do. There must be a way around this death and chaos. There always is. We have to find it."

Mamduh took a sip from his tea and spoke quietly. "Each time he enters another underworld, he must face a challenge to complete a ritual. The journey takes time to complete. But if he should be interrupted during the time…" Mamduh sat and mumbled for a moment as if he ran the ritual through his mind. "It is the sixth hour in which the most significant event in the underworld occurs. The soul of Ra unites with his body. This event is the point at which the sun begins its regeneration. It is a moment of great significance but also danger."

Colin squinted at Mamduh. "So, is there a set time for that part?"

Mamduh replied, "Midnight. That part of the ritual must be performed during the veil, changing from night to day. You must wait till he starts to enter the sixth world. That is when the mummy will be the most vulnerable."

Dominic rubbed his hands together and spoke. "Midnight it is. That's when we storm the castle."

Bree rolled her eyes. "This isn't a fairy tale, Dom. This is serious. There must be a way out of the throne room before all the death and destruction."

Mamduh raised his hand. "I do not want Miss Moira hurt. She is like a daughter to us all."

Dominic took Mamduh's hand. "I vow I will see her to safety." He squeezed it once for emphasis.

Mamduh nodded. "I believe you. You are her warrior. Whatever her next journey is, it will be as the Gods intended. I will pray for your success."

Mamduh rose. "I shall leave you to your thoughts. Good rest to you all." He moved out the doorway as the group left sat to riddle the impossible—how to get out safely.

Dominic worried about Evie but, more importantly, Moira. He feared what Pierre would do to her or what he might have already done. Moira played Pierre's obsession off as mere rivalry, but Dominic knew men like Pierre. When it came to Moira, Pierre had a more sinister goal in mind.

Ewan's voice broke the silence. "The portal. It's the only way out besides the entrance." He glanced around the campfire. "Well, we must go back to the twenty-first century anyway. Why not have Evie open the portal, and we all go home?"

Dominic stood and started to pace.

Bree turned to him. "Dom, what is it?"

Dominic stopped, ran his hand through his hair, started speaking, and then paced again. He puffed and strode away from the group, standing a short distance away, looking out over the Valley of the Kings.

Colin came beside him, staring as well. "It's Moira ye are puzzling over. The destruction is likely the throne room imploding. The death ye fear may be Moira's since ye have to figure out how to get her out of the throne room safely, then ye go back in the throne room in time to make the portal before ye suspect the place will fall, right?"

Dominic ran his hands through his hair. "Yes and no. It's more complicated than that."

Colin barked a laugh. "It's never easy, and with the Fae, it's always complicated."

Dominic stared out over the horizon. All he could think of was Moira.

Colin stood next to him, quiet.

Dominic exhaled. He needed help, and Colin was

the most experienced with the portals. If he told him all, could he help? Colin made it work with his sister, Ainslie. Could he help Dominic with the puzzle by figuring out how to beat the mummy, get Moira out, and make the portal, keeping them both safe?

Colin spoke lowly. "I recognize that look. If ye are thinking of staying in the past for a woman, think again. Ye'll break Bree's heart. I've had to leave a loved one behind before, and it's not easy."

He sighed. "I asked Moira to come through the portal to the future."

Colin sighed. "Complications from true love. It always comes down to this." He stared out over the land. "At least ye won't hurt Bree's feelings, wanting to stay here."

Dominic toed the sand. "Moira said no, that she needed to stay here. But I know her fate here. It was on the wall of the museum. If she stays, she will disappear soon."

Colin slowly turned, staring at Dominic. "Explain what the museum wall said about her disappearance."

Dominic rubbed his forehead and tried to recall all it said.

"After the last dig, she disappears." Ewan's voice came from behind them.

Colin and Dominic turned in unison as Ewan walked toward them. "It's the dig we all fell into from the portal. They never find her again. Pierre tries to claim her work, but the villagers, Nubi and Mamduh, don't allow it. She gets credited with the job, and they finish it in her name."

Ewan moved closer to them. "I read the wall often when Evie wanted to see the eye."

Colin rubbed his neck and glanced between Dominic and Ewan. "Maybe she's meant to come, and maybe not. It's hard to tell. The Fae fable doesn't have anything to do with a woman. It's two fighting brothers." He exhaled. "I don't know if she's meant to stay or come. It usually takes a stone to travel the portals, but we all came through the eye without one."

Dominic squinted at Ewan. "You and Evie spoke of the stone and the quotes the first night we were here. The night you both woke me. Was there more you discussed?"

Ewan nodded, and then he jumped a little. "The statue, the Divine Family Statue. Evie thinks it has something to do with this. With the Stone of Hope."

Colin turned to Dominic. "So, go get the damned statue."

Dominic shook his head.

Colin held his hand up. "Wait, let me guess. Pierre has it. Damn, nothing is ever easy. I think Brigid does this to me on purpose."

Ewan grabbed his father's hand. "Da, the statue is with Pierre. Evie is with Pierre. She'll find it. I'm sure of it."

****

Moira's guard escorted her to the largest tent in the encampment. She snorted. It had to be Pierre's tent. The guard opened the tent flap and waved her inside. The tent appeared empty as she walked in. The guard grinned and let the flap fall, leaving her alone. She turned, lifted the flap, and bent to exit, only to run into the back of the guard who stood directly outside the tent. He grunted over his shoulder as she returned to the tent. Moira couldn't waste any time. Pierre would likely

161

be here soon. She frantically searched for a weapon, a knife, a gun, something she could use.

She spied the Divine Family Statue on the table and gasped. Could she secret it away from Pierre?

She glanced around and spied a scarf, but as she grabbed it, the tent flap opened, and Pierre made his entrance as she flung the scarf over the statue.

"Ahh, my dear, we meet again." Moira glared at her enemy and hated him even more. He smiled back so smugly.

Tilting her head back, she spoke. "Where is Evie? What have you done with her?"

He held the Ankh up between them. "I finally have the power I've always wanted."

Moira barked a laugh and backed up against the table, letting her hands slowly travel behind her, trying to find a weapon. "You don't have any power. The mummy only has power when he's close to the Eye of Ra."

Pierre lowered the cross and moved to her.

She backed sideways down the table with her hands behind her, still trying to find a weapon. "Evie, the girl. Please tell me she is safe."

Pierre grinned. "She is safe, I promise. I wouldn't hurt a child. You should know this, Moira."

Moira released a sigh, hoping he'd treated Evie well.

Pierre set the Ankh on the table and drew closer to Moira. "You will tell me how to harness the power of the cross for the mummy. He asked for the cross, so it must have some significance to wielding his power."

Moira stopped at the end of the table by the tent wall. She had nowhere to go as he backed her into a corner.

She lifted her eyes to Pierre. "I don't know what you are talking about. How about you ask the dead man yourself?"

Pierre slashed his hand out and yelled. "*Mensonges! Lies!* I know you interpreted hieroglyphics for your uncle. I want the rejuvenation ritual. One for the dead to become not only alive but immortal. Your uncle talked about it…a lot." Pierre crossed closer and ran his finger down her cheek. "Certainly. You can recall that?"

Moira shook. He was so close; she hated it when he did that. It turned her stomach.

Shaking her head, she replied. "I don't recall."

Pierre grabbed her arm, dragging her to the center of the tent. "You will do what I demand, Moira. Or the *môme brat* gets it." He flung her to her knees.

Moira glared at Pierre. "You just said you wouldn't hurt her."

Pierre let go of her arm as he studied her for a moment. He grinned as he turned and poured himself a cup of wine.

He stood, surveying her as he drank. "I'll do what is necessary to get what I want." He sipped again as he eyed her over the cup.

Moira stared at the ground. The ritual, she hadn't thought about it in years. Her uncle was more versed in the ceremony and had studied it intently for as long as she could recall. Moira needed to remember the order and then find some way to stop Pierre and the mummy.

Pierre's voice was quiet yet forceful. "The ritual, Moira. What does it entail?"

Moira glanced at him and then back at the ground.

God, it had been years since she thought about the Book of the Dead, and she hadn't ever actually seen it. She had only read about it from hieroglyphics on a wall in the Temple of Edfu. Moira would have to recall the details. Midnight, the Ankh, and the throne room with the Eye were all she could remember. There was a scuffle in the sand as Pierre stepped toward her.

She called out, "I am trying to remember. It's been years, and I didn't record it. My uncle did." She turned to him. "And if he did, you have his notes, not me. You can look it up."

Pierre nodded. "What do you remember now?"

Moira knew she had to give him something. Even a little tidbit, and he'd take it and be satisfied. "Midnight, the Ankh and the Eye of Ra. That's all I remember."

The tent flap opened. Two of the army of the dead men came into the room.

One spoke in Arabic. "You are summoned. Bring the Ankh."

Pierre grabbed Moira, and she pulled back.

The army of the dead man looked at her, then Pierre. "Only you, not the woman."

Pierre held her hard against him. "She knows what to do with the Ankh."

"Only you, not the woman."

Pierre grabbed the Ankh, his movement causing the scarf to fall from the Divine Family Statue.

Pierre chuckled. "I have the cross now. The *môme brat* and the mummy will get me all the riches of Egypt."

His eyes went to the Divine Family Statue. "Keep your little statue, Moira." He held up the cross. "I will have it all anyway."

Pierre turned and followed the sandman out of the tent.

Moira curled over herself with a sigh.

She rose and crossed to the Divine Family Statue, wanting to hide it in case Pierre changed his mind.

She knew she wore an undershirt, but the dress could do little to hide something like this. The statue was gold but hollow. Suppose she could tie it to her. She picked up the scarf and quickly grabbed the figure. Moira wrapped the scarf around her middle, keeping the statue at her lower stomach. If anyone noticed, she could hunch over with a fake stomach cramp. She tied off the scarf and set the dress down when the tent flap flipped open, and one of Pierre's thugs smiled when Moira raised her head.

He grabbed and dragged her from the tent across the encampment to another. The brute dragged her into the tent and dumped her on the ground.

She stood up, trying to fight as the guards stepped back from her. "Fine, just drop me here. See if I care."

"Moira?"

Moira whipped around at the small voice. "Evie?"

Moira waved to Evie to stay seated and waited for the guards to exit the tent when she bent over and lifted her skirt.

Evie gasped and rose as Moira shook her head. "I am not injured, but I have something." She grinned as she unwound the scarf and pulled out the Divine Family Statue. She held it up between them. "At least I got my statue back."

Evie stepped across the small space and into Moira's arms. "God, I am so glad ye are here, that someone is here."

Moira held her close. "I'm sorry, Evie. Please tell me they are treating you well." She held her at arm's length to get a good look at her. She wore typical Egyptian woman's clothing, much the same as what Moira wore, but white, a dress with no headscarf. Moira hated Egyptian clothing and typically opted for her pants and button-down shirt, which was easier to move around in.

Evie nodded and turned, sitting on the cot. "They are nice to me after I threw a fit to ensure I'd have all the comforts." She sighed. "Except I am a prisoner forced to call on my powers at Pierre's whim."

As Moira sat next to her, Evie peeked at her. "I am sorry about the army. They didn't hurt anyone, did they?"

Moira patted her leg and lied. "No, they didn't hurt anyone. Just grabbed me and the village's sacred Ankh, a cross. Then came back here."

Moira examined the tent. The one cot seemed nice and was well covered. Evie had a table with a lamp and a few fruits and dates sitting out. Next to them was an ornate carafe, which she suspected contained juice.

She walked to the table, set the statue down, filled a cup with liquid, and placed a date into her mouth. As the fruit burst, she thought of Dom. She hoped he was okay. The last she saw of him, he was held between two army of the dead men who beat him.

She took a sip from the cup, coughing. "They gave you watered-down wine?"

Evie giggled. "Aye, I've had wine before. Da lets us on special occasions."

Moira hmphed and took a healthy gulp, then ate another date. She was hungry.

Evie glanced down, then back at Moira. "What will happen now? I mean, what will Mr. P do with us?"

Moira filled her cup again, drank it all, and then filled it again.

She took another sip from her cup and glanced at Evie. "You called him Mr. P." She laughed. "I like that. Mr. P sounds so…unimportant."

Evie shrugged. "Well, we call Mrs. Abernathy Mrs. A, and she's really important, but I won't call him by his name." Evie hugged herself and shivered.

Moira crossed and sat next to Evie. "I suspect he will leave you alone, but for me. Ha! I am certain he has some special plans for me."

Evie sighed.

Moira wrapped her arms around her. "Don't worry. I have dealt with Pierre for many years. I can deal with him again."

The tent flap opened, and Moira stood before the Divine Family Statue, hoping it was enough to hide it. She mentally cursed herself. She should have hidden it immediately. The guard handed her a worn leather-bound book wrapped around by a leather tie. She regarded the book as many memories crashed into her mind at once.

Her uncle sat in a chair with the book on his knee, carefully drawing. He held it up to a wall, comparing symbols, and then turned to look at her with a smile.

The guard shoved it in her hands and turned, leaving the tent.

She stood silent, holding the last memory of her uncle, of her family, and a sob escaped before she knew it. She clutched the book to her chest and held it like her lost family as tears gathered.

Evie's voice broke into her thoughts. "What's that?"

She blinked rapidly and crossed to the cot and sat beside Evie as she held out the book. "This is my uncle's. In it is all his work, his entire life."

Moira carefully untied the leather and opened it to the ribbon, marking the last dig they worked on. Pierre had it this whole time and never once opened it. She smirked. He wouldn't know what to do with what was inside, anyway. She lifted it to her face and took one long sniff. The smell from her uncle's cigars was faint but still there. She breathed in the scent—how she missed him.

Evie looked over Moira's shoulder as Moira flipped the pages backward to the dig of Thutmose III in the Valley of the Kings.

Evie leaned over, looking at the book. "What are ye looking for?"

Moira glanced at Evie, then back at the book. "Pierre stole the Ankh." She studied Evie, who blinked blankly back, reminding her the child didn't know as much as she did.

Excitement filled her. To share her vast knowledge was something she craved. "It's a cross, a sacred Egyptian cross."

She turned page after page, trying to find the one she wanted, and spoke as she searched. "He wants to use it to make the mummy more powerful. I suspect making him immortal by using the ritual of the Amduat. It's the nightly journey of the sun God Ra through the twelve regions of the netherworld."

She turned the pages again and pointed her finger at the book. "Ahh, here he is, Thutmose III, in the

Valley of the Kings." Memories of her and her uncle working in the tomb flooded her mind. She saw the wide grin of her uncle's face at the thrill of discovery, the camaraderie of interpreting the ceremony together from the hieroglyphics to the sense of accomplishment when they cataloged the finds.

She sighed. "That's where we found the earliest complete version of the Amduat. In the tomb of Thutmose III in the Valley of the Kings. The pharaohs believed the spirit made this journey to the twelve different underworlds and undergo the Weighing of the Heart ceremony, where their purity would determine whether they would be allowed to enter the Kingdom of Osiris. Which is what they consider the land of the dead."

Evie gazed at Moira. "Like our Heaven?"

Moira nodded. "Something like that, yes. Egyptologists believe that if the dead followed this path again through the netherworld, the dead would become undead and immortal. The Ankh shall carry him to the netherworld to permit him inside each world so he may complete the journey, thus completing the ritual of immortality. If someone breaks the ritual, chaos shall ensue, and death will befall everyone around."

Evie snorted. "I don't think the mummy can do that."

Moira spoke as she read, "Well, I suspect not either. But Pierre believes he can, and after what I have seen since you and your uncle came through the portal, I might believe it."

Evie smiled. "My family came through the portal. I know they are on their way here to save us."

Moira stopped and peered at Evie. She took a deep

breath and regarded the child. If she asked about Dom, what all could the girl tell her? "Your uncle, Dom, what is he like?"

Evie grinned at her. "Ye like him, don't ye?"

Moira gazed down and blushed. Was she that transparent?

Evie cleared her throat and sat up straighter. "Dom is the best uncle ever. Well, my only uncle, but still."

Moira turned to face Evie as she continued. "You know he saw you. Or a picture of you in the museum. That's why I opened the portal. He wanted to see you." Evie glanced down. "The Eye of Ra never did anything except show me a picture. I didn't think it would be a portal."

Moira patted her knee. "I know, honey. It was an accident."

Evie hummed. "Uncle Dom, well, he's in the military. They call it special ops. It means he's top secret and does hazardous missions for the United States Air Force. He flies planes, and he can't talk about the missions he does. But he claims he's saved the world more than once."

Moira's eyebrows rose. She knew he was skilled, but this was more than she thought.

Evie sat back on the cot, getting comfortable. She obviously liked talking about her favorite uncle. "After Mom's run-in with the bad Fae, Uncle Dom promised to be more involved in our lives. He's visited often, and we were in his home city when I opened the portal."

Moira picked at her dress.

If she asked outright, would the child know? "Does he have a girlfriend or anything like that?"

Evie giggled. "Not that I know of. He's always

been busy with the military."

She took Moira's hand. "When he saw ye in the portal, he said ye were beautiful."

Moira blushed and patted Evie's hand. "Thank you, Evie." She sighed. "I found the dig, but I still have to find the page on the ritual, or Pierre could really mess it up."

As Evie rose and crossed to the Divine Family Statue, Moira bent back to her uncle's notebook. "I'm glad ye got it back." Moira hummed her response as Evie studied the statue.

"Moira?" Moira glimpsed up as Evie fingered Horus' figure on the statue. "He has an eagle head."

Moira hummed. "Horus and Isis flank Osiris' bust. Horus is their son and the God of sun. He's always shown with an eagle head."

Evie yawned. "That's why yer story talked about eagles?"

"In part, yes, but it was also about the division of power, the resolution of who ruled what part." She bent back to her uncle's book, intent on studying the ritual of making the mummy immortal. There had to be a way to stop the ceremony without all the chaos and death. She just had to find it.

Evie yawned as Moira studied the book. "Why don't you try to get some sleep."

Evie nodded, crossed to the cot, lay down, and covered herself with the blanket.

Once tucked in, Evie spoke in a sleepy voice, "I'm glad ye're here, Moira. And that Uncle Dom likes ye."

Moira smiled. "Me too."

Chapter 15

"The temple is built over the believed location of the fight between Horus and Seth, where Horus defeated Seth for ruling the kingdoms. The modern Arabic name, Edfu, comes from the ancient Egyptian name 'Djeba.' 'Djeba' means Retribution Town, where they brought Horus' enemies to justice," Moira spoke lowly to Evie as two army of the dead guards escorted them to the Edfu temple. With it nearing midnight, Pierre lit up the place, likely costing a fortune in rental equipment. Her uncle always said Pierre was wasteful, but if he wanted the ritual of Amduat, it needed to occur at midnight when the veil between the worlds was thinnest.

Evie whispered back, "He brought me here a couple of days ago." She glanced up. "When he made me unleash the army." Evie sighed. "I'm sorry."

Moira hugged the youth as they walked along. "No worries, Evie. And I suspect the mummy had more to do with raising the army than you."

Uncle Ben's voice echoed in Moira's head as they approached the building—spoken from long ago but felt so nearby. His deep baritone rumbled as the rasp from smoking too many cigars spread warmth at the memory. "The focal point of the temple exterior is the entrance gate. Monumental in scale, the twin columns measure an impressive 118 feet tall. The incised reliefs depict Ptolemy XII smiting his enemies before Horus." Her uncle had slashed his hand down, emphasizing smiting. "This part of the structure was visible to the public, and literacy levels were nonexistent—only an elite few could read and write hieroglyphics. They used this as propaganda to emphasize the might and legitimacy of the rulers." The last he'd said with a laugh, and Moira smiled at the memory.

They progressed into the entryway, and the familiar etchings greeted Moira, reminding her of happier times. She and her uncle working together to discover the lost treasures of Egypt. Nostalgia overcame her, but she shook it off. She needed to be on her toes, alert. With the magic of the pharaoh combined with the magic of the Fae Dominic spoke of, Moira had to examine as much as she could to find a way to stop the power of the mummy. So far, all she'd seen was if the pharaoh lost focus during the ritual, it would break the connection, and the ceremony would stop. But there was a risk—chaos and death. She smirked, recalling her uncle speaking of "propaganda to emphasize the might and legitimacy of the rulers." Every threat always came the same: death and chaos. It left Moira wondering if it ever happened that way.

Evie tugged on her arm. "The eagle statue, it's important?"

Moira bent, murmuring, "Yes. This is the granite statue of Horus as a falcon wearing the double crown of Upper and Lower Egypt, where the populace would bring their offerings in this outer courtyard."

Evie hissed, "But those who have hope will renew their strength. They will run and not grow weary; they will walk and not be faint; they will soar like wings on eagles."

Moira muttered, "The quote from the Divine Family story that matches The Stone of Hope fable. Dominic said you saw a long rectangle gem that's green and broken in half."

She bent, speaking faster as they walked farther into the temple. "The ritual. I found the weakest point. It's when he enters the sixth realm. So be ready."

They strode on as Moira spoke lowly. "I still haven't figured out how the Stone of Hope plays into this. It has to be part of the ritual, and I suspect it's in the hieroglyphics on the wall, but there are literally thousands here." She sighed. "My uncle and I never got the chance to interpret them all. That would take a lifetime."

Evie nodded as she hugged the Divine Family Statue close to her. Moira thought it strange that Evie insisted on bringing it. How she hugged it may have helped her cope with this impossible situation. At least it ensured the statue stayed with them so Moira could keep the valuable relic.

The sandman led them into the throne room and onto the wooden platform over the throne, which sat some twelve feet below them. The large golden Eye of Ra glittered in the lights from the opposite wall behind the throne.

Evie turned away with her eyes shut.

Pierre stood in the center at the edge. When they came alongside, Moira spied the mummy of Psusennes I as he sat on the throne.

When they approached, Pierre turned. "Ah, Moira, my sweet."

He reached for her, but she backed away closer to

Evie.

He tsked, his French accent heavy and mocking. "You should celebrate with me on this wonderful occasion—to witness the Ritual of Amduat in person. Why, there is no other find that can rival this."

The mummy held up the Ankh and spoke in his deep, gravelly voice. "You will chant the ritual for me so I may enter each world and on into immortality."

Pierre turned to Moira and raised an eyebrow.

Moira folded her arms. "I'll not help you. Speak it yourself."

Pierre grabbed her arm. "You know I cannot read hieroglyphics." He twisted her arm till she cried out. "Do it, Moira."

She shook her head as she spied Evie, keeping her face turned away from the Eye of Ra. Moira's heart went out to her. If she stared at it, she'd power this eye as well.

Pierre laughed. "It's good we brought the *môme brat*." He nodded to a sandman. "Grab her. Hold her at knifepoint."

Evie cried out as the man from the army of the dead held her with a knife at her throat.

Moira stepped forward, but Pierre pulled her back against him. "Read, my darling."

Her gaze shot to Evie, worry over the child consuming her. "Evie. Keep your eyes closed, and I'll get us out of this."

Evie nodded and held the statue close, backing away till she bumped into a sandman.

Moira's gaze rose to the wall where the twelve papyrus columns that symbolized the concept of Amduat, the nightly journey of the sun God Ra through the twelve regions of the netherworld, were displayed.

Her uncle's voice echoed in her head, and she repeated what her memory showed her. "It is believed that if the spirit followed this path through the netherworld, the dead would become undead and immortal. The Ankh shall carry him to the netherworld to permit him inside each world so he may complete the journey, thus completing the ritual to immortality."

She turned and glared at Pierre. "If you break the ritual, then chaos shall ensure, and death to all around."

Pierre laughed. "You sound like Ben, your uncle. Save the threats." He twisted her arm again. "Read the wall. Start the ritual!"

Moira turned and began reading. First, the words came in old Egyptian from the hieroglyphics, and her uncle's voice echoed as she slowly read. "*Ana au un ne peta enta.*"

Pierre shoved her. "English, Moira."

She snorted. "It begins with the Invocation of Divine Entity."

Moira read from the symbols the interpretation coming easier the farther she went. "If you are in Heaven or on Earth. In the south or the north. Or the west or the east. I am the only one in your body. I am the pure one of eye. Not shall I die a second time. My moment is in your body. All forms are my habitation. I am he who is not known. I am the unveiled."

The light in the room faded, and they stood in pitch blackness regardless of the electrical lights.

The mummy's voice echoed ethereally. "The ritual has begun."

The light slowly rose in the room. The pharaoh's wrappings were perfectly white, like new. He had already begun the change from dead to mortal, and it was only the start. It was all happening too fast.

Pierre nudged Moira. "Read it, my dear."

Moira lifted her gaze, finding the next symbols. "In stage one, the sun God enters the *akhet* or western horizon, a transition between day and night."

She turned to Pierre. "There's no turning back now, Mr. P. Chaos and death will be your end."

He grabbed her and kissed her. "No, my darling. I will have all. You and the riches of Egypt."

****

Dominic followed Colin while Bree and Ewan stayed behind him. "Colin, are you sure this is the way?"

Colin laughed. "If the lights lighting up the night sky like a beacon don't tell ye we head to something, then ye need more military training."

Dominic stifled a laugh. "It's usually not so obvious." He chuckled. "Pierre is dumb."

Bree leaned forward as they crept through the outer courtyard. "Pierre may be stupid, but I bet the mummy isn't."

Colin leaned around Dominic, pointing to Bree. "Ye will stay out of it, Bree. Let Dom and me do the fighting this time."

She smirked. "I can't stay out of it. I'm the bait, remember? He thinks I'm his sister, his wife. I'm the distraction that will stop the ritual. Then you and my brother can do all the fighting you want."

She turned to Ewan. "You stay back."

Ewan grinned as they cleared the entrance to the hall leading to the throne room. "Me? I plan to stay out of it and watch. This is gonna be better than any movie.

A mummy brought to life to become immortal. A stupid Frenchman as the bad guy. A damsel in distress whom Uncle Dom, the military junkie, must save. And Evie will use her Fae magic powers. All I need is popcorn and a soda."

Colin and Bree stopped, turning in unison to Ewan as they wore equal deadpan expressions.

Colin brought his finger up to his son's face. "Stay out of it."

Dominic almost laughed aloud. Bree's kids were entertaining. It made him wonder if his kids would be the same. He shook himself. Wow, he'd never thought of having his own kids until now. But he liked the thought.

The lights went out, and echoes of voices came down the hall.

Colin whispered, "Silence from this point on. I'll lead."

Bree muttered, "Please, God, let us find my baby all right."

Ewan spoke softly, "Evie says she's fine but scared. I told her we're coming."

Colin sighed. "Wait, I thought you only felt each other? Another power? Ye both speak in yer minds. Brigid and I will be having a little chat when we return."

Ewan grunted. "Only when we are close can we mind speak. Brigid can do it from far away."

Colin growled, "The fairy gets it when we return."

Bree shushed them both.

As they approached the opening, the lights faded back on, resembling the sun rising as Moira's voice carried to them. "In stages two and three, he passes through an abundant watery world called 'Wernes' and the 'Waters of Osiris'."

Colin stepped forward, and Dominic grabbed his arm. "You must wait for stage six. Remember when the spirit comes, and he is at his weakest point. Then we distract and attack."

****

Moira shifted as Pierre's grip loosened. If she kept his focus on the mummy, then she might be able to search for a sign or anything having to do with the Stone of Hope. As the ritual stages unfolded, she scanned the symbols on the wall. The Egyptians had an incredible ability to foretell the future. Too often, she'd seen a story told on the wall come to pass in life in the present. While they were all written in the past, an illustration of the rectangular stone would be on the walls if the magic Fae stone had any power here. As long as she stalled Pierre for time to search, she had hope. She just had to find the green stone.

The sound of water rushing filled the chamber as Pierre gasped. "What the hell is this?" The pharaoh raised his arms, calling out as water rose around him. Pierre moved back as the rising water splashed below. The sandman holding Evie at knifepoint lowered his knife, and they both shifted back. Evie kept her head turned and eyes shut.

Moira turned to him. "The next stages. He must pass through an abundant watery world."

The waters covered most of the golden eye as Pierre cried out, "He won't drown, will he?"

Evie turned to Pierre, her eyes open. "He's dead, ye dummy. He can't die till she brings him back to life."

Moira's eyes connected with Evie's, who eyed Pierre. When he turned toward the pharaoh, Evie mouthed, "Dom comes to rescue us."

As Evie winked, Moira's eyes went wide, and a sigh escaped. Soon, this would end. She hoped for the best as she scanned the wall for a square green stone. It had to be here. There were too many coincidences for it not to be.

The waters receded. With his wrapping partially removed, the pharaoh's skin peeked between the remaining wrappings. The skin between returned to a glowing, healthy pink. The rejuvenation had begun. Moira needed to find the Stone of Hope and fast.

Pierre shook her arm. "Read the next one."

Moira refocused on the wall with the Amduat, finding her place again. "In stage four, the pharaoh reaches Imhet. The difficult sandy realm of Seker, the underworld hawk deity, where he encounters dark zigzag pathways which he has to navigate as they drag him on a snake-boat."

A ghostlike boat appeared as a flying hawk pulled it along. The pharaoh climbed in and bounced along as the ship crossed the rough, ghostlike sands. When he swerved this way and that, sand flew up hitting them on the platform.

Pierre jumped back, releasing Moira, who sidestepped and refocused on the other symbols. The magic stone had to be here somewhere. She followed the opposite wall, only reading about the worship practices and how the enemies of Horus met their end.

Pierre grabbed her and brought her forward to the edge of the platform. "You aren't paying attention. He awaits the next reading." When Moira's gaze moved to the pharaoh, the sand boat and hawk had faded, and he stood fully restored to a human, wearing his jeweled necklace and loincloth, looking alive and real. Time was not on her side today. Moira needed to find out how the Stone of Hope connected to this soon.

Moira pulled her arm from his grip. "I read ahead." She waved her hand to the walls. "To interpret this without a key is difficult. If you are so impatient, *you* do it."

Her gaze found Evie's, who had turned facing Moira's side, her face away from the eye as she held the Divine Family Statue before her with a smile. Her guard, no longer holding her, stood at attention behind her. Good. Pierre and the sandman had lost focus. Now, to get on with it and, hopefully, the end.

Moira turned to the wall bearing the Amduat ritual, her eyes trailing to her last place. "In stage five, the pharaoh discovers the tomb of Osiris, which is an enclosure where beneath is a hidden lake of fire."

Pierre turned to her, yelling, "*Feu? Fire?*"

Moira shrugged. "The four elements of the world. Earth, water, fire, and the last—wind."

Her memory flashed of Dominic's warning about a swirling wind where there weren't any signals of another presence meant that Fae powers were close. Her eyes connected with Evie, who grinned.

As the chamber beneath them burst into flames, the mummy raised his hands and screamed.

Pierre leaped back from the platform's edge along with the others, avoiding the flames. But Moira stood her ground. She must continue her search for the symbol of the stone.

Her focus went back to her last place on the ritual

wall. "In the sixth stage, the *ba*, or soul of Ra, unites with his body. This event is the point at which the sun begins its regeneration."

Moira's focus went inward as she recalled her uncle's notes. The sixth stage was the most significant event in the underworld. It occurred at a moment of great significance but also danger. The mummy's soul must enter his physical body to regenerate. If he doesn't, he will not become mortal and unable to continue to the immortal part of the ritual. His final goal—immortality. Confident that Mamduh had told the others of the ritual, Moira banked that this was it, the place where Dominic would interrupt.

Her gaze flew to the symbols on the wall. *Damn, it's too soon.* Moira hadn't found how the Stone of Hope played into the ritual, into the present. But she kept searching. It was there, and all she had to do was find it.

Chapter 16

Dominic crept behind Colin as they came to the opening of the throne room. The shadows of light danced on the walls like flames. Was the place on fire?

The light receded as Moira spoke from beside Pierre. "In the sixth stage, the *ba*, or soul of Ra, unites with his body. This event is the point at which the sun begins its regeneration."

This was it, the sixth stage. Colin slid into the room. From their place in the center edge of the platform, Evie turned as her eyes connected with her father's. She gasped as Colin put his finger to his lips. Dominic came close behind. Evie smiled wide and bent her head, closing her eyes.

A wind whistled through the chamber, and a ghostlike figure flew overhead. Pierre spoke with wonder. "His spirit returns. Once connected, he will be mortal, and the rejuvenation part will be complete. Then we begin the immortal stage."

Bree and Ewan followed Dominic, but his focus was on Moira who stood beside that damned Frenchman.

The pharaoh yelled from the throne, "Mutnedjmet! My wife's here, in the flesh! My men, get her!"

Colin turned, and his gaze landed on Bree and Ewan entering the room. "Damn it, woman, why can't ye do as ye are told! It's too early!"

The sandman next to Evie stepped forward grabbing Bree as Pierre turned and yelled, "You!"

As Evie ducked left moving around her guard, Pierre turned back to the pharaoh, yelling, "My king, you must stay focused!" The spirit circled above the mummy but didn't descend as the wind swelled in the chamber.

The pharaoh called out, "My army, attack!"

The sandman dragged Bree to the right edge of the platform as she fought him. Colin went after Bree as more of the army of the dead men entered the throne room. As Colin fought them, they shifted to the far left rear corner of the platform in a jumble of fighting bodies.

Dominic moved toward Moira near the center, but sandmen crowded her, forcing him to fight by hand, the proximity too close for any gunfire. He might have hit Moira or the kids. As he punched another sandman, Evie and Ewan traveled left through his periphery toward the far side of the platform descending a ladder to the throne room's floor. Evie held the Divine Family Statue close to her. What were those two up to?

****

Evie went down the ladder as her brother followed. "What do ye mean, the statue needs to be down here? Down here is where the bad guy is. We don't want to be closer, Evie!"

She stepped off the last step into the sand. "It's here, Ewan, the stone. I feel it, but I can't find it."

Ewan shifted off the last rung and grabbed the statue. "Let me hold this, and ye go look for the stone."

Evie tugged it back. "No, I have to hold the statue."

Ewan grabbed it again. "No, I'll hold it. Ye go

184

look."

Evie pulled as Ewan yanked in a short tug of war. Both stopped as their eyes connected over the statue, speaking in unison, "Siblings arguing over the stone."

Ewan jumped. "It's us! We find the stone!"

Evie grabbed the statue from Ewan, and something rattled inside. Her gaze flew to Ewan as she held out the statue. "Eagle's wings! Horus is the eagle. It's in here!"

Ewan grabbed the statue. "We must break it open!" *Whack!* He hit it against the ladder, breaking the wood.

Evie barked. "It's gold but hollow."

Ewan knelt on the floor, grabbing a rock and beating the statue. *Whack!* The first hit bent the gold. *Whack!* He hit it again, this time folding it in half. He roared as he hit it yet again. *Whack!* It twisted and then broke at the base with a clank.

They each grabbed a gold piece and held it up as a green glittering stone fell from each side. Two halves of a square sat on the sand floor.

Ewan's eyes connected with hers. "Evie, ye must mend the stone!"

****

Moira kept reading the walls, desperately seeking anything to do with a stone. She turned back as Dominic punched another sandman, who staggered back as another filled his spot. Dominic hit the one to his right. She glanced Colin's way. More sandmen swarmed Colin as he tried to get to Bree, who huddled against the far right wall.

When Moira turned back to the wall, her eyes landed on a series of stories that featured colored stones using magical powers. That was something she'd never seen on any wall in Egypt before. The kids said the

Stone of Hope was a green rectangular stone. Moira scanned the stories, trying to find the green rectangle. Her eyes traveled fast over the symbols. First was a red heart that vanquished a foe in a sea of dead bodies rising from graves. Her gaze moved on. Next was a purple oval. Nope. The following story featured a black rectangle. She had to find the green stone.

Dominic struck a sandman. "Colin, I can't get free of them!"

Colin punched one and yelled back, "Me either." He hit one and called out, "Something has got to change."

Moira searched again.

Pierre grabbed her arm, spinning her to him. "*Mon Dieu. My God,* Moira, the pharaoh's losing focus. He must complete the sixth stage and move on." He shook her. "Do something."

Her head fell back, and she noticed a series of hieroglyphics on the ceiling.

An image of the throne room was above including a platform. Two smaller figures stood next to the king on the throne. In the next scene, they held their hands over their head as each held a square jewel. In the third scene, the smaller figure held the gem up, and it was whole—a whole square. In the next scene, the gem was in a person's hand atop the platform, and a light shot from the stone to the king on the throne. In the last scene, the king fell dead, and the inscription read, "The magic stone shall banish evil and bring hope to all the people in Egypt." Hope! This was it! But where was the stone?

Evie's scream came from the floor of the throne room. "Moira! I have it! The stone!"

Moira peered over the edge, and Evie held the stone up, just like the image above her.

Pierre shook her. "Do something!"

Moira glared at him. "I am, but you must let me go!"

She yanked her arms from him and peered over the platform, her arms out. "Evie, here! Toss it here! I know what to do!"

Evie's gaze connected with hers, and she nodded. She drew her arm back and pitched the stone to Moira.

For Moira, everything went in slow motion.

The green stone tumbled toward her, the gem glittering in the light. The mummy moaned as the spirit flew overhead. Her eyes stayed on the gem as the sounds of fighting echoed in the chamber. She must catch the stone.

Dominic yelled out in pain, but her focus stayed on the green stone. As the jewel came closer, her hands reached out farther. When it rose close enough, her hands closed over the gem, and a pulse of energy shot through her. She held the stone before her as she focused on the pharaoh.

She gathered all her energy like Dom said. Her love for her uncle. Her desperation to bring Egypt to the people. Her last thought on Dominic and her feelings for him. She balled all these feelings into one, and with all her might, she screamed at the top of her lungs, "The hope of the righteous is gladness. The expectation of the wicked perishes."

Light shot from the stone into the mummy, forcing a roar at the contact. The spirit floating above screamed at a high pitch, hurting Moira's ears, but she held firm. She had to—to save them all. The wind swirled harder as the light from her arms pulsed.

The spirit flew around Pierre, who yelled, "No, what? No, not me!"

The spirit circled Pierre, picking him up as the ceiling opened a hole to the dark sky above.

The pharaoh yelled out again, "The Gods call for you, Pierre! Your death will deliver hope to Egypt!"

As the spirit held Pierre, they flew into the mummy, carrying him with them as they flew through the ceiling out into the blackness of the night in one last echoing yell.

The light faded, and Moira fell to her knees, clutching the stone to her chest. The men from the army of the dead burst into puffs of sand that fell to the floor.

Moira drew a breath, then another. Strong arms grabbed her shoulders. She jolted away as she turned, fearing Pierre had returned.

Her eyes connected with Dominic's. "Moira, are you all right?"

She launched into his arms. "Dom!" His arms encircled her, holding her tight.

Colin helped Bree up from the floor. "Bree, are ye okay?" She nodded.

Evie called from the floor. "Ma, Da, ye okay?" Colin and Bree stepped to the edge of the platform and peered down.

Moira followed their gaze, and Evie and Ewan stood, each holding half of the Divine Family Statue.

Evie grinned at them. "I found it, Da! I found the stone."

Colin nodded. "Aye, that ye did!"

Colin's eyes moved to Moira, who held the long green rectangular stone up in the light. "I'll be damned.

It was in the statue this whole time."

Dominic loosened his grip but kept her in his arms. "What happened to the mummy? To Pierre?"

Moira glanced at the ceiling, then Dominic. "Sent to the underworld." She pointed at the hieroglyphics as she spoke. "I didn't notice it before. My uncle and I only focused on the Amduat ritual. But it shows the stone and the power sending the evil to the underworld here."

Dominic grunted. "And the army of the dead with them."

Moira's eyes connected with his. "I did it. The good thoughts worked, and the wicked, well, died like the curse said."

Colin sighed. "Good riddance." He held his hand to her. "The stone, Moira?" She handed it to him, glad to pass it along, her arms still tingled with energy—the stone's power, a near frightening experience.

The twins came up the ladder, first Ewan and then Evie.

Bree rushed to them, taking both into her arms. "My babies. Are you both okay?" They hugged her back.

Ewan stepped back. "Did ye see the spirit take the mummy? Wasn't that awesome!"

Evie held on to her mom, keeping her face turned from the Eye of Ra. "Mom, I'm so glad ye are here."

Bree held her close as she ran her hands up and down her back. "Me too, Evie."

Colin held the stone as he focused on Dominic. "What happened with the chaos and death? Was that it?"

A rumble sounded throughout the room as

everyone froze. One of the large pillars fell across the throne room, crushing the throne. The sound of rocks falling and tumbling filled the chamber as the platform shifted.

Dominic's glare shot to Colin. "You had to say something, didn't you?"

Moira called out, "The mummy's curse. The room will collapse. We must get out!"

Dominic held her tight. "Not till I know Colin, Bree, and the kids are safely into the portal."

Colin took Bree and Evie into his arms. "Ewan, come to me!"

Ewan rushed into his father's arms as the platform shifted again.

Colin knelt before Evie. "It's time, Evie. Ye must open the portal to get us home."

Bree held her. "Be brave, Evie. You can do this."

Ewan patted her shoulder. "Ye got this, sis."

Evie held her hands out like before and stared directly into the Eye of Ra. The wind swirled hard and fast as the eye spun. The gray center faded into a room filled with Egyptian antiquities. Colin started down the ladder, but Evie called out, "No, Da, just jump toward the eye."

The chamber rocked again. And Moira called out, "Dom!" He held her tightly.

Colin took Bree's and Ewan's hands. "Ready. Jump!" They leaped toward the eye, and the swirling mass sucked them in.

Ewan stood on the other side. "Evie!"

She shook her head. "Dominic and Moira first!"

****

Evie tried to hold the portal, but the power was too

much. She couldn't control it this long. She felt the power drain, the portal close.

Ewan screamed again. "Evie, the portal's closing!" Her gaze connected with her brother's in the portal. Tears streamed down his face. "Come through now! Please!"

She pushed her energy harder, trying to keep the portal open for Uncle Dom and Moira.

She pulled more, and the energy rose on its own.

Her dream boy's voice came to her. *~I have it, Evie. Ye go on through. ~*

She turned, and her dream boy stood beside her, his arms out with energy, keeping the portal open.

He grinned as his voice sounded in her mind. *~Go, Evie, go to safety. I'll ensure yer uncle and Moira make it. ~*

Evie blinked as the pull shifted to him. "Will I see ye again?"

He smiled. *~Look for me in yer dreams, Evie. I'll be there. ~*

Evie cried out, "Whose name do I call for in my dreams?

As the portal sucked her through, the boy whispered, *~Aodhán, call for Aodhán. ~*

****

Dominic's time grew short. Colin, Bree, and Ewan had already gone through to the other side. Evie followed as the portal remained open, but for how long?

Moira tugged away from Dominic. "I must stay. You go."

He shook his head as he pulled her arm. "Come with me! I love you!"

She pulled from his grasp and turned to the

doorway leading out. The chamber shook again as rocks fell, blocking her exit.

Dominic grabbed her and swung her into his arms, carrying her. "Wrong way. Your future is this direction." With Moira in his arms, Dominic launched from the platform into the eye as the chamber rocked, and the ceiling fell, crushing the platform.

Chapter 17

Dominic gripped Moira as they fell to the ground, landing in a tangle of arms and legs. Dominic held her tightly momentarily as she sensed his breath rushing out.

He murmured, "I've got you, Moira. I've got you, love." He shifted back till their eyes connected, and his hand brushed her hair from her face as he smiled.

Bree rushed to them, helping them up. "Dominic, don't scare me like that again! I almost thought you didn't make it!" Bree tugged his arm as he helped Moira stand.

Moira blinked as her gaze roamed the room they'd landed in. Egyptian artifacts surrounded them. The larger ones sat out while the smaller ones were in glass display cases.

Dominic followed her gaze. "The room is bigger now, and more items are here."

Moira glanced at him and then back at the items.

Her eyes caught the large sarcophagus. She moved to it as she gasped. "Wait, this is Thutmose III from the Valley of the Kings." Her hand ran over the top. "My uncle and I discovered this." Her face lifted to Dominic's. "But Pierre stole this and sold it to the highest bidder."

A group of children crowded into the room, followed by their teacher. "Now, students, don't touch anything. This room is my favorite in the whole museum."

A girl came up beside Moira. "Cool, a mummy's coffin!"

A boy came up beside her. "Mmmmmmmmmm!" She shoved him, and they moved to the next item. The children walked around looking at each item, some commenting. Colin, Bree, Ewan, and Evie shifted toward the door but didn't leave.

Dominic took her hand. "Moira, come this way."

She backed up but refused to leave the room. Her gaze focused on the display as she started to read it. It spoke of her finds, each and every one of them credited to her and her uncle—the latter ones only to her. It mentioned her uncle and his death, a heart attack, not a stabbing. Egyptian Historical Society and Egyptians involved in searching and keeping the history of Egypt available for everyone mourned his loss. She teared up again, thinking of her uncle, and breathed deeply.

Before she read more, the teacher called out, "Students! Everyone, gather around." The teacher stood before the display beside the Eye of Ra, and it was the first time Moira noticed it. In front of her stood a life-sized black-and-white photo of her she recognized. It was the one where she stood on the pyramid of Giza that her uncle had taken. She wore her nice dress and had her hair styled up unlike now where her usual unruly curls escaped. Her eyes teared as her hand moved to her chest, and her breath caught.

The teacher smiled. "Moira Joanna White was a famed archeologist, and thanks to her foundation, we have all these great artifacts to study and learn from." Moira's critical eye scanned the room, searching each artifact, identifying each and every dig Pierre stole from her. Yet, the items all sat in full display before her.

A student raised their hand. "What happened to her?"

The teacher glimpsed at the picture and then back at the student. "Well, this is the most curious part of her story. She worked on a dig in the Valley of the Kings, and it imploded. When they excavated it, they never found her body. What makes it odder is her rival in the race to uncover Egyptian artifacts disappeared in the same dig."

The teacher paused, allowing the children to absorb what she'd said. She crossed to the casket and stood beside it. "Some say she ran off with the man. But others aren't quite convinced. You see, the pharaoh she dug up had a curse." She paused and smirked. "So, did she run off, or did the mummy's curse get her and take her to the underworld?" She banged on the coffin's side. The loud sound echoed in the room, making all the kids squeal.

The teacher laughed as Dominic chuckled beside Moira as a smile came over her face.

The teacher crossed and stood staring at her picture. "After her disappearance, her workers formed The Moira White Foundation. Using the money from the finder's fees, they created a workforce that continues her and her uncle's work to place many of Egypt's greatest historical treasures in museums worldwide. If it weren't for her, none of this would be here. If it weren't for her, the Egyptian Historical Society wouldn't know so much about the pharaohs or that time." She turned, facing the students. "Her foundation works to this day in digs all over Egypt."

The teacher moved on. "Come along, kids. The Scottish display is next and just as historically important." The kids filed out, some stopping to touch one last item or stare at her photo.

A young girl stood before her image and tilted her head. "Moira Joanna White." She sighed. "I wanna be just like her."

The teacher called out, "Kylie, come on. Don't dawdle!" The girl ran out of the room, leaving Moira speechless.

Ewan strode to the display. "I'll be damned. It's changed." He turned and waved at the room. "Look at all this stuff. It's three times more than was here before."

Colin barked, "Ewan, language." He laughed. "Aww, hell. I agree. I'll be damned."

Bree bent to Evie. "Honey, you're looking at the eye, and nothing happens."

Evie shook her head. "I don't feel the pull anymore." She turned to her mother. "It doesn't call me."

Colin strode by, flipped the Stone of Hope in the air, and caught it. "Of course not, sweetie. We got the Stone of Hope. Mission complete."

Ewan turned to Moira. "But what does this mean now? Moira's in the future. What will she do?"

Moira's gaze traveled the room again as her eyes teared. All the items, once lost, were now together in a place where the world would benefit, and people would learn about the life of the Egyptians in the past.

Her eyes connected with Dominic's as he smiled. "I know the perfect thing."

****

A few months later, in Dominic's home in Miami, Florida, Moira rushed into his office with a package. "It's here, Dom! Mamduh's grandson had it made and sent." She ripped the tape, opened the box, and dug into the stuffing.

It turned out that after she and Pierre disappeared, Mamduh and Nubi went to the Egyptian courts and filed to have her findings refiled under her name instead of Pierre's. They worked for years, trying to recover all the artifacts that Pierre sold. Some, but not all, were purchased or donated for the greater good of education. Those who donated the priceless items were rewarded as esteemed donors and listed as high-level contributors to the Egyptian Historical Foundation.

She pulled out an Ankh. Memories of her and Dominic traveling to New Gourna, Egypt, on honeymoon came rushing back, making her eyes tear up.

The village, now years later, had developed into a bustling mini-city. The Moira White Foundation was a huge success within the archeological world.

A man resembling Mamduh approached her with a wide grin on his face. "My grandfather spoke of this day. Promised the whole of the village you were alive in the future."

He embraced her, and tears gathered in her eyes. "You can't be Mamduh."

The man shook his head. "I am Mamduh's grandson, named after my father and grandfather. It's an honor, Moira White."

Moira glanced at Dominic and back at Mamduh. "I can't be Moira White. She died."

Mamduh shook his head as he led her through the

village toward the rock which held the Ankh for the town. "My grandfather claimed the Gods took you for a greater duty. He said the Gods determined your fate long before. Now, you only serve the Gods by bringing the knowledge of Egypt to the future. To our future."

A woman approached and handed Mamduh a wrapped item. He grinned as he took it. "My wife, Edwa."

The woman grinned as she bowed. "We have prayed for your arrival for some time. We are honored you are here."

Arriving at the place where the sacred Ankh was displayed, many villagers collected around.

Mamduh held the wrapped item to his forehead and whispered a prayer. He turned and handed it to her. "We carried on you and your uncle's work. It is time we return it to its owner."

Moira opened the fabric, and her uncle's notebook sat in her hands. Tears fell as she brought it to her chest, then to her nose, and she smelled her uncle's cigar smoke. Memories of them together flashed in her mind.

Mamduh called out over the village, "Miss White, the Gods have returned her to us! Answering our prayers!"

She turned to Dominic, who wrapped his arm around her and smiled. "You deserve all of this and more, Moira."

The memory faded as the cross glittered before her.

She held it up, showing Dominic, who shivered when he spied it. "Don't care if it's a replica. It still gives me chills."

Moira shifted it in the sunlight and turned it

around, examining the work. "It's so perfect. I almost can't tell if this is the real one or not."

Dominic backed up. "Please tell me that's the replica, wife."

She set it aside. "Yes, it is. And it will look perfect with the other artifacts we work to find for the tour."

Dominic took her in his arms. "Wife, I like the way that sounds." He kissed her full on the lips.

Husband and wife. Her wedding day came back to her. Dominic had stood before the Eye of Ra in the Egyptian wing of the museum in Georgia. It was the last day of the tour before the display proceeded to its permanent home, the Miami Florida Museum of History, where Moira planned many lectures and visits.

The museum staff had cleared most of the artifacts, which they'd already packed for the next move, leaving the room open for their special day.

She brushed her hand down her gown, a tea-length dress with a silk rose undergown and an antiqued white lace overlay. She felt like the perfect bride. Dominic stood tall in his black suit with no tie. It turned out ties were a hazard for combat, and he hated wearing them anyway.

Evie and Ewan served as escorts. Ewan carried the rings on a pillow and Evie a basket with rose petals. They proceeded down the aisle, each focused on their duty. Ewan held the pillow steady even though a ribbon kept the rings in place. Evie tossed rose petals right and left as they proceeded her. When they arrived at Dominic, he winked at them, and they turned and sat in the front seats beside Bree.

Colin agreed to give her away and walk with her down the aisle.

Margaret Izard

He patted her hand. "Are ye sure ye want to marry this rogue? There's still time to run away."

Moira blushed. "I'll have him today, tomorrow, and even on Sunday."

Colin winked at her as he arrived before Dominic and handed her off.

Dominic took her hands in his and held them. A pastor conducted the short wedding ceremony. They exchanged vows, and before Moira knew it, Dominic had her bent over his arm, kissing her senselessly as the crowd cheered.

She shook off the memory and glanced at the clock. "Dom, you will be late. Don't *you* teach fighter pilots today?"

Dominic grinned. "Why yes, I do. Going to take them out in one-on-one combat." He rubbed his hands. "I will teach them the art of war."

He stopped smiling at her. "Little miss college professor. Don't *you* have a class to get to?"

Moira beamed at the new title, a college professor. Inspired by Mamduh's grandson's claims, Dominic's connections gave her all the needed documents to live a typical life in America. He even had the University of Miami give her an honorary PhD, claiming she was the long-lost descendant of Moira White. Their story claimed Mamduh's and Nubi's descendants raised her, ensuring she was involved in all the digs from her adulthood to date. Her knowledge and expertise in Egyptian history were now well-known throughout the world.

He took her in his arms. "Tell me, wife, if you had to do it all over again, would you?"

Moira wrapped her arms around his neck. "The

Eye of Ra, time travel, defeating Pierre and the evil mummy, or finding my true love?"

Dominic kissed her. "Well, finding your love." He kissed her again. "Bree said the Fae fable did say, 'If his heart was true, he could look into the eye, see his destiny, and fate would reward him.' "

Moira grinned. "Has fate rewarded you, husband?"

Dominic smiled. "Yes, I found my true love."

Moira sighed. "Yes, and I found mine."

****

Bree curled into Colin's embrace as they sat at their favorite spot, the couch in the study before the blazing fire at Dunstaffnage Castle a few days after their return to Scotland, nearly three months after the trip through time to Egypt. They'd completed the museum tour only to detour for Dominic and Moira's wedding. He exhaled. Thank God Dom decided to come to the future and not stay in the past.

Colin took a sip from his whisky glass and swallowed it, the burn reminding him of everything he had yet to do. The Stone of Hope needed to be returned to the chapel. He'd have to confront Brigid about the kids' powers and find out what he could do to help them. Colin had missed an extra month at the law firm, passing it off to his assistant, who won the case alone, impressing Colin. He'd likely have to promote the man.

Bree tapped his arm. "I've asked you twice. When will you return the Stone of Hope?"

"Tomorrow afternoon. I suspect Dagda will show, seeing as how it's Brigid I want to have a word with."

He exhaled as he swirled his whisky glass. "The kids' powers. What will we do now?"

Bree sipped her wine. "What we've always done,

Colin. Love and support them." She sat up. "Have hope, Colin. The kids will be fine."

He nodded. "They do tend to care for themselves more and more. I just worry if they will become more involved in the other stones' recovery."

Bree hugged him. "I suspect they will. There will be a day when Ewan will take on the guardianship duties. At least this time, he'll be informed, unlike you. He'll do fine."

Colin kissed her head. "I hope so."

****

Colin sat in the Chapel in the Woods. A whoosh of air came through the building despite the fact the door was closed. Footfalls sounded, and someone sat beside him on the pew. He reached for the whisky decanter and glass, poured a generous amount nearly to the rim, and handed it to the man beside him.

Dagda took the glass and lifted it for a heavy swig. He swished the liquid around his mouth, then swallowed and groaned. "Colin, yer whisky gets better every time I sample it."

The king of the good Fae took another hardy sip and swallowed before he spoke. "The Stone of Hope?"

Colin held it out to him. The green gem winked in the sun's rays that filtered through the windows.

Dagda took it and pocketed the stone.

Colin exhaled, thinking of Bree, his true love, happy that her brother had decided to come to the future with them. "At least this time, we didn't lose anyone to true love."

Taking another sip, Dagda moaned, then spoke softly. "Ye didn't, that's true."

Colin glanced at his longtime friend, and the Fae's

202

expression stopped him. "What, what is it?"

Dagda sighed. "There's news from the Fae realm. Balor is dead."

Colin sat up. "Dead? I thought ye couldn't kill each other?" He reached for his glass, filled it, and took a swig. Balor, the king of the evil Fae, dead? Bree's tormentor finally met justice. He toasted the pulpit, mentally thanking God, and drank again.

Dagda's voice came hard. "I wouldn't be toasting yer God yet, Colin. His realm has a new ruler. His youngest son."

Colin sat and thought for a moment. The memory of his dream hit him: the dream, the dragon shifters, Balor's sons. "Wait, Balor's sons are the dragon shapeshifters. Ye said they served the good Fae."

Dagda nodded and waved to the whisky decanter.

Colin filled his glass.

Dagda took another gulp. "Aye, they do. Live here in yer realm." He regarded his glass. "As time passes, the old continue to age, while the young grow."

Colin smirked. "Ye are immortal. What is this growing old?"

Dagda sighed. "We can get old, ye know. It takes longer than ye." He took another sip. "Balor's youngest now rules the Fomoire Fae. If ye thought Balor was evil, this one's worse. Hotheaded, young, and powerful." He sighed. "Even more powerful than my grandson, who was born the most powerful Fae to exist." He gulped the whisky. "Be on alert. Three stones are still not found, and the new king is a power-hungry little ass."

Colin sat up. "Ye have a grandson? Congratulations! Morrigan's or Brigid's?"

Dagda smiled wide. "Brigid's. She's with him now. Got himself in a little trouble."

Colin nodded. "Kids do that." He turned. "And speaking of Brigid, why do my kids have more powers than originally thought? What the hell is she doing with them?"

Dagda took a swig of his whisky. "Fae powers in humans are a fickle thing. Sometimes, they sit dormant, doing nothing. Other times, they grow as the human grows." His gaze met Colin's. "Ye should be thanking Brigid for taking them into her training. The growth of powers without guidance leads to evil. Unknown powers suddenly found within a human can be— unpredictable. This way, yer kids have a fighting chance."

Colin sipped his whisky. "A fighting chance at what?"

Dagda uttered, "Their future."

Dagda stood and tossed the Stone of Hope in the air. The gemstone stayed suspended in the center of the chapel. He waved his hand, and the stone floated to the open box beneath the window for Hope. The stone rested, and the box faded from view.

Every time a stone found its home, Colin felt a sense of relief. For him, it signaled the closing of another chapter in a long book. Satisfied, but not totally—his duty demanded that he search for the other stones, Doubt, Faith, and Destiny.

Tilting his glass, finishing his drink, Dagda handed the glass to Colin as he waved and faded. "Thanks for the tot, Colin."

Colin stood. "Wait, how will I know who the new king is? What does he look like?"

Dagda's voice echoed in the chapel. "Ye will know just by the presence of his evil. Ye will know."

Epilogue

The next day, near dusk, Evie sat in the Chapel in the Woods at Dunstaffnage Castle. She flicked her wrist again, and nothing happened. That was the thousandth time Evie had tried to call Aodhán to her—her dream Fae boy. She flicked her wrist again, and a pain shot through her wrist.

She cried out and slammed her hand on the pew. "Damn it!"

She stood, closed her eyes, and screamed as loudly as possible. "Aodhán, where are ye?"

When she opened her eyes, her brother Ewan stood at the back of the chapel.

She puffed as she turned and sat back down as footfalls came closer. Evie bent her head as she wiped a tear from her eye.

Ewan sat next to her on the pew. "Ye call him again?"

Evie nodded as tears gathered in her eyes.

Ewan breathed. "He still doesn't come, this dream boy of yers."

Evie blurted out, "He's real, I know it!"

Ewan took her hand in his. "Evie, I know he's real. I know how important he is to ye." When she lifted her gaze, his connected with hers. Her brother's sympathetic expression broke her heart. The reality hit. Her Fae dream boy wasn't coming back.

Ewan took her in his arms, making new tears fall. "It's okay, Evie. Powerful Fae or not. He wasn't good enough for my sis." He patted her back. "There will be other boys, Evie." He released her and handed her a handkerchief. Like all his others, a small embroidered cursive ERM sat in the corner.

She dried her tears and sat up a bit. Other boys, sure, there would be many.

She offered the hanky back, and Ewan waved at it. "Ye keep it."

She pocketed the square, and they both sat silently as they sometimes did.

After a time, Ewan spoke softly. "I saw him, yer Fae."

She turned her head. "When? I thought no one saw him."

Ewan's eyes connected with hers. "When he held the portal open so ye could come through."

Aodhán had held the portal for her and saved her again, as he'd helped her from the start. His kiss still tingled on her lips, and her hand went there.

Evie tilted her head. "Well, at least one person saw him. I'm not totally insane."

Ewan sighed. "No, Evie, ye aren't insane. But he looked a lot like Brigid, don't ye think?"

Evie shrugged, not wanting to think of the Fae dream boy who came no more, breaking her heart.

Ewan shoved her shoulder with his. "Mrs. A made cookies."

Evie shoved back. "What flavor?"

Ewan smiled. "Chocolate chip."

Evie smirked back. "Race ye."

Both teens jumped up and took off from the chapel,

running to the castle.

****

They'd left the chapel door open.

Beside it, Aodhán materialized and closed the wooden door. "One day, Evie, we'll meet again. I promise."

Brigid strode to him. "Come, son, the Fae council awaits to determine yer punishment for sneaking into the human realm."

Both faded from the chapel.

A word about the author...

Margaret Izard is a multi-award-winning author of historical fantasy and paranormal romance novels. She spent her early years through college to adulthood dedicated to dance, theater, and performing. Over the years, she developed a love for great storytelling in different mediums. She does not waste a good story, be it movement, the spoken, or the written word. She discovered historical romance novels in middle school, which combined her passion for romance, drama, and fantasy. She writes exciting plot lines, steamy love scenes and always falls for a strong male with a soft heart. She lives in Houston, Texas, with her husband and adult triplets and loves to hear from readers.

You can email me at

info@margaretizardauthor.com

www.margaretizardauthor.com

Thank you for purchasing
this publication of The Wild Rose Press, Inc.

For questions or more information
contact us at
info@thewildrosepress.com.

The Wild Rose Press, Inc.
www.thewildrosepress.com